FROM THE
NANCY DREW FILES

THE CASE: Nancy investigates the death threat and a suspicious series of accidents plaguing a popular teen talk-show host.

CONTACT: Nancy's friend Susan Ling is working as an intern on the "Marcy!" show, and Nancy's working to save Marcy's life.

SUSPECTS: Vic Molina—*the TV producer is Marcy's ex-boyfriend. When it comes to the business of payback, he's a prime-time player.*

Karen Kristoff—*the young magazine editor not only wants to start her own talk show, but also hopes to knock the competition off the air . . . for good.*

Jack Cole—*Marcy's stage manager is looking for romance. If he doesn't find it, he may start looking for revenge.*

COMPLICATIONS: Talk about hatred. Talk about deceit. Talk about danger. There's all that and more on the set of the "Marcy!" show. Nancy has to find a way to protect the perfect target: a celebrity in the spotlight.

D0198055

Books in The Nancy Drew Files® Series

Available from ARCHWAY Paperbacks

The
Nancy Drew
Files™

Case 86
Let's Talk Terror
Carolyn Keene

AN ARCHWAY PAPERBACK
Published by POCKET BOOKS
New York   London   Toronto   Sydney   Tokyo   Singapore

AN ARCHWAY PAPERBACK *Original*

An Archway Paperback published by
POCKET BOOKS, a division of Simon & Schuster Inc.
1230 Avenue of the Americas, New York, NY 10020

Copyright © 1993 by Simon & Schuster Inc.
Produced by Mega-Books of New York, Inc.

All rights reserved, including the right to reproduce
this book or portions thereof in any form whatsoever.
For information address Pocket Books, 1230 Avenue
of the Americas, New York, NY 10020

ISBN: 0-671-79478-7

First Archway Paperback printing August 1993

10 9 8 7 6 5 4 3 2 1

NANCY DREW, AN ARCHWAY PAPERBACK and colophon
are registered trademarks of Simon & Schuster Inc.

THE NANCY DREW FILES is a trademark
of Simon & Schuster Inc.

Cover art by Tricia Zimic

Printed in the U.S.A.

IL 6+

Chapter
One

"Look, Nancy—there's the Chicago Media Center!"

Keeping a close eye on the Eisenhower Expressway traffic as she drove, Nancy Drew glanced ahead and to the left. Her friend George Fayne was pointing to a distant metal and glass skyscraper thrusting up into the Chicago skyline.

"We're so lucky!" George's brown eyes sparkled with excitement. "Here it is an ordinary Monday afternoon, but soon we'll be in the TV audience of 'Marcy!' waving to Bess at home."

Bess Marvin was George's cousin, and George's and Nancy's best friend. "Poor Bess," Nancy said. "I know she's brokenhearted about missing this trip."

"Bess is the biggest Marcy Robbins fan of all time," George added. "Did you know she used to subscribe to *Teen Talk* magazine, just to read Marcy's column?

"Oh, well." George shook her head ruefully and then shrugged her slender, athletic shoulders. "At least having the flu gives Bess an excuse to watch 'Marcy!' every day."

"We'll have to be sure to get Marcy's autograph for Bess," Nancy said, pulling onto the ramp for the JFK Expressway. She turned the air conditioner up to high. It was a hot, humid day, one of Chicago's famous August dog days. "We should be there in just a minute, George."

"It was terrific of Susan to invite us to stay with her," George said. Susan Ling had gone to high school with Nancy and George and was now an assistant on the "Marcy!" show. "We don't even know how long we'll have to stay."

"Just until we find out who's been sending Marcy threatening messages. Maybe we'll get lucky and solve the case very quickly," Nancy said.

The girls had reached the heart of downtown Chicago, known as the Loop. Nancy could see the grand old facade of the Wrigley Building as they crossed under the elevated train tracks. Off to her left was the Sears Tower, the tallest building in the world. Nancy scanned the office buildings as they made their way to Lake

Shore Drive, with its magnificent view of Lake Michigan. "Here's the Media Center," she said finally.

"And there's Susan!" George said. "She's standing by the entrance."

Nancy pulled her blue Mustang up to the curb and tooted the horn. A slender, dark-haired girl carrying a large white envelope turned around, a questioning look in her pretty brown eyes. Seeing Nancy and George, she hurried over to the car, smiling warmly. "You're right on time," she said. "Just leave the car here. I'll call a valet to park it."

"A valet?" Nancy asked, surprised. She shut off the engine.

"This is real VIP treatment," George said, climbing out and joining Nancy on the sidewalk.

"Well, you're Very Important People to me," Susan said with a laugh. "Besides, I'm the one who's responsible for the show's parking arrangements. It's part of my job as a general gofer. You know, go fer this, go fer that."

"Well, it's great having friends in high places," Nancy quipped, and handed her car keys to the valet who appeared at Susan's wave as they approached the lobby.

Once they were inside, Nancy looked up. The soaring vaulted ceiling made the center seem immense. Twenty-foot silk flags, hung from high up, announced coming events at the center.

"These girls are with me," Susan told the balding, freckled security guard. "They're guests of Marcy Robbins."

With a smile, he handed Nancy a pen for her to sign in.

"Are you going to see the show?" he asked, pointing to a set of double doors marked Studio A—"Marcy!" A laminated silhouette of a wavy-haired young woman holding a microphone was prominently displayed next to the doors.

"I'm taking them to the offices first," Susan answered for Nancy and George. "They'll get to the set from backstage."

"Okay," the guard said, giving Nancy and George two stiff cardboard passes. "You'll need these in that case."

"The audience members get tickets," Susan explained. "These passes are for the offices."

Susan led Nancy and George through a cordoned-off part of the lobby beyond the elevator banks. "Too bad Bess isn't here," Susan said. "She'd love the topic of today's show—'Is calendar modeling sexist?' And we've got male calendar models as guests."

"Bess will definitely watch at home," George assured Susan with a grin.

Nancy pointed to the envelope Susan was carrying. "Is that a calendar?" she asked.

"No," Susan said. "This is Marcy's new publicity shot. Want to see it?" She stopped just long enough to open the envelope and pull out an 11-by-14 color photo.

The photo was of a petite, freckled-faced Marcy Robbins standing in front of a studio audience wearing a houndstooth-check jumper with a white blouse and bright green tie. Marcy's expression communicated both intelligence and lively fun.

"What a great photo," Nancy said. "And she looks so young. If Bess hadn't told me she was twenty-six, I'd have thought Marcy was no more than eighteen."

Susan smiled. "Marcy hasn't seen the photo yet. I just picked it up for her, and now I have to drop it off at her office."

"Great!" George said brightly. "That means we can see her office."

Susan led them through a set of double doors marked Stern Productions at the back of the lobby. "This is where we work," she said, pulling the door open.

The first thing Nancy and George saw was the receptionist, a blond woman seated behind an enormous glass and chrome desk.

"Hi, Ginger." Susan waved to the woman. "These are old friends from high school, Nancy and George." Susan breezed through the reception area and pushed through another door. "Marcy's office is right back here," she said, leading Nancy and George down the hall, into a large white office decorated with furniture in vivid primary colors.

"This is fabulous," Nancy remarked, taking in all the photos of celebrities and the framed awards that lined the walls.

"Marcy has great taste," Susan agreed.

"Hi!" called a male voice. A slender guy of about twenty-five with brown hair popped out from beside a file cabinet in the corner of the office. His yellow shirt emphasized his pale skin and small, light-colored eyes. He had a walkie-talkie in a special holster on his belt.

"Jack!" Susan said, sounding surprised. "What are you doing here?"

"Marcy wanted a back issue of *Teen Talk* to use as a prop," he said, holding out a rolled-up magazine in one hand. "When she was writing for the magazine, she did an article about one of the models on today's show."

"Guys, this is Jack Cole, our production stage manager," Susan told the girls.

"Hi," Nancy said, offering her hand.

Jack didn't respond, though. He was staring past Nancy at the doorway, his eyes round with surprise. Nancy spun around.

In the doorway stood a petite young woman with a scrubbed, freckled face. Her hair was in curlers, and a clear plastic cape hung from her shoulders. For a split second Nancy didn't recognize the famous Marcy Robbins. "Jack, I'm waiting," Marcy said with slight impatience. Her normal bubbliness was missing.

"Yes, Queen Marcy," Jack replied with a joking grin, handing her the magazine. "I've been busy getting the other props milady requested. Give me a break, okay?"

"Sorry," Marcy replied wearily, turning to Susan. "Meet me in my dressing room, Susan," she said, heading up the corridor.

"I'm out of here, too," Jack said, pulling on his work gloves.

"See you," Susan said with a quick wave as he left the office. Then she turned to Nancy and George. "I'll introduce you to Marcy now."

When they got to Marcy's dressing room Nancy was surprised at how small it was. Bright track lighting made it warm and friendly, and cards from well-wishers filled a bulletin board on one wall. On another wall stood a long rack filled with clothing. The other two walls were all mirrors.

In the center of the room, Marcy sat in a beautician's chair, her eyes squeezed shut and a copy of *Teen Talk* on her lap. Behind her, a dark-haired, middle-aged woman in a pink smock yanked rollers from Marcy's hair.

"Hey, take it easy, Dee," the talk show host

said, wincing. "And keep it simple today. Forget the barrettes."

Nancy knew something was bothering Marcy Robbins.

Marcy looked up at Susan, Nancy, and George just then. "Oh, hi," she said as if seeing them for the first time. "Sorry, it's crazy today. But then, it's crazy every day."

"Marcy, this is George Fayne and Nancy Drew, my friends from River Heights," Susan told her.

Marcy's eyes lit briefly on George, then fixed on Nancy. "Thanks for coming, both of you," she said.

Scrunching her face and peering in the mirror, she suddenly jerked her head around. "That's enough. Thanks, Dee. Tell Midge I'm ready for makeup."

"You could use more combing out," Dee argued, though Marcy's hairdo looked perfect to Nancy.

"That's okay. It's only hair," Marcy said, dismissing Dee. When the hairdresser left the room, Marcy leaned forward. "I didn't want to say anything in front of Dee. Susan has told me all about the investigating you've done, and I was really impressed." She bit her lip and went on.

"This show means everything to me, and I couldn't bear to lose it. Not this way, anyhow.

I know I've made a few waves, but I *believe* in making waves. I want to help people communicate better. That's what 'Marcy!' is all about. I was prepared for some people not to like me. But threats?" Marcy tilted her head and blew out a deep breath.

"How many threats have you received?" Nancy asked gently.

"Just two," Marcy replied. "They were slightly garbled messages on my voice mail telling me to quit the show or else."

"Can we hear them?" Nancy asked.

"Sorry," Marcy said with a regretful shrug. "I erased them immediately. The *last* thing I need around me right now is negative energy."

"What could you tell from the voices?" George asked. "Were they male or female?"

"I couldn't tell," Marcy replied. "They were disguised with some sort of electronic distortion. The sound was scary." She pounded her fist on the arm of the chair. "Just when everything was going so well, too!"

"Does anyone else know about the threats?" Nancy asked.

Marcy shook her head. "Just Susan and you two." Marcy quickly changed the subject, as if she were anxious to push the threats out of her mind. "By the way, Susan, did you pick up my new publicity shot?"

"I put it on your desk," Susan said.

Marcy glanced at the clock on the wall. "I still have time to look at it," she said. "Go get it, okay?"

Marcy turned to Nancy and George and explained, "The *Tribune* is doing a two-page spread on me, and they need the new shot today. I can't wait to see it."

"Here it is," Susan said, waving the envelope as she hurried back into the room. Smiling, Marcy reached for the envelope and opened it. Her smile vanished as she withdrew her empty hand and peered inside.

"What is it?" Nancy asked, reacting to the expression on Marcy's face.

"I'm not sure," Marcy murmured, turning the envelope upside down and giving it a shake.

Torn pieces of paper fell onto the magazine on her lap. Someone had just ripped Marcy Robbins's brand-new publicity photo to shreds!

Chapter

Two

M<small>Y PICTURE</small>!" Marcy cried, the color draining from her face. "It's totally destroyed!"

"I don't know who did this to you, Marcy," Nancy told her, "but we're going to do our best to find out. Right, George?"

George agreed by nodding.

Marcy slid the torn pieces back into the envelope and held it out to Susan. "Get rid of this," she said. "I never want to see it again."

"That photo had to have been torn in the past few minutes," Nancy pointed out. "Who exactly has access to your office?"

"Why, anybody who works on the show," Marcy answered with a helpless shrug. "I don't lock my door every time I leave."

"All right, everybody out!" a stout, gray-haired woman in a white smock announced, marching into the room. "Ten minutes to show time, Marcy. We're late."

Marcy took a deep breath and exhaled it noisily. "I have to get myself together. I have a show to do."

Setting a satchel down on the vanity countertop, Midge began taking out bottles of foundation, brushes, makeup pencils, and mascara wands.

"Let's talk after the show," Marcy called to Nancy and the others at the door. Then she obediently turned her face toward the makeup sponge and added, "Susan, make sure Nancy and George are seated down center."

"Yes, yes, Susan will take care of everything," Midge kidded. "Goodbye, everyone."

"I don't know how Marcy can function after something like that," George said when they were out in the hallway.

"It's horrible," Susan agreed, "but Marcy is a pro, and she won't let anything interfere with her performance. Come on, I'll show you where to sit."

"Susan," Nancy said, lightly touching her friend on the arm. "Keep the pieces of that photo in a safe place, will you? I want to look at them after the show."

"Behind you," came the sound of a masculine voice. Nancy turned as two handsome, muscular young men, dressed casually in chinos and cotton sweaters, came striding up the hall. Judging by their obvious good looks, they had to be the calendar models, Nancy decided.

Nancy and George exchanged a grin as Susan introduced herself and her friends. "You're Bill and Joe, right?" she said, extending a hand to greet them. "I'm Susan, Marcy's assistant. I was just going to look for you so I could show you where to go. This is Nancy and George."

"Bill O'Donnell," the model with jet black hair said, shaking Susan's hand and nodding to Nancy and George. Nancy noticed that his gorgeous dark eyes lingered on her, and she felt heat rushing to her cheeks.

"Nice to meet you all," the other model said. "I'm Joe Spiro."

"Backstage is right this way," Susan said, leading them down the corridor to a set of double doors with an unlit red bulb over it. "When the light up there is on, it means they're taping," she explained. After punching in a code on a digital pad next to the doors, Susan led them into the semidarkened backstage area.

"You guys can wait here in these chairs until Marcy calls you out," Susan said.

When the models had disappeared, Susan reached into her pocket and pulled out two tickets. "These are for you. Just go down those steps at the side of the stage, and the usher will seat you. See you after the show."

"Where will you be, Susan?" George asked.

"I'll be watching on a monitor while I confirm guest bookings for the rest of the week— one of my many jobs," she added with a wink.

Susan hurried off toward the offices while Nancy and George made their way into the packed auditorium. All around them, the audience buzzed in happy anticipation. Onstage Nancy noticed two bright blue sofas with red and yellow coffee tables in front of them. A TelePrompTer was hung overhead.

"It looks so different on TV," George said.

A dark-skinned woman in a red dress walked onstage, holding a headset in her hands. "Hi, everyone," she said greeting the crowd. "Thanks for coming to 'Marcy!' I'm Brenda Fox, assistant to the producers, and I want you all to know that Marcy is real easy to talk with. So don't be nervous if she asks you something," she advised. "And if you've got a strong opinion, come on out with it! That's what 'Marcy!' is all about."

"This is so cool!" George whispered to Nancy.

Ms. Fox held up a finger and paused to listen to her headset. "Okay, we're ready, folks," she said after a moment. "Counting, five, four, three, two—and rolling!"

Bright lights and music came on, and suddenly Marcy Robbins was onstage, with the audience applauding wildly.

"You're so nice! Hi, I'm Marcy Robbins, and this is 'Marcy!'" The music ended, and Marcy seated herself on one of the sofas. "Today I have a treat for you! We have some top male models with us. They're gorgeous and they make big bucks—when they're working, that is. But they may not be what you expect! We'll meet Bill and Joe right after these messages."

"She seems so relaxed," Nancy said as a large monitor on one side of the stage began showing the commercials that the audience at home was watching.

Onstage Marcy leaned forward and waved to some people in the audience. "How you doing? Having fun?" she asked. Then she turned to the stagehands and said something that made them laugh, though Nancy didn't hear what it was.

The makeup artist Nancy had seen backstage trotted on and began dabbing Marcy's face with a sponge, while the hairdresser adjusted a stray curl of Marcy's auburn hair. When the monitor showed the station logo, Jack, the production stage manager, appeared at the side of the stage. "Five seconds," he announced.

"We're back," Marcy said brightly. "And now, meet Bill and Joe. Fellas, can you come on out here?"

The audience applauded, and a few people whistled as Bill and Joe filed onstage and sat down. "Here they are," Marcy said. "And aren't they gorgeous. Could you tell us a little about yourselves and how you got started as calendar models?"

Joe explained that he was a former fast-food restaurant manager from Pittsburgh. Bill had been a highly paid model since he was a child.

"I work to support my mother and little sister," Joe said with a shrug. "For me, modeling is just a job, like any other."

"That's not how I feel at all," Bill said. "I love my work! It's totally glamorous. And I love the money I can make doing it."

"These guys are selling their images, so that women will drool over them. What do *you* think about that? Is this sexist? Is it exploitation?" Marcy ambled toward the audience and pointed her microphone at George.

"Well," George began, sounding slightly nervous, "it's not hurting anyone. I think it's okay."

"Just okay? I think it's fantastic, Marcy," a girl behind George piped up. "Why shouldn't girls have a chance to appreciate good-looking guys?"

"This is *more* than appreciating, isn't it? It's ogling!" Marcy said. "And a lot of people say it hurts everyone. Some even say it's immoral! What do *you* think?"

Nancy realized Marcy was zeroing in on her. "I don't know about immoral," Nancy said. "To me, it's—well, kind of silly."

That comment drew an unexpected laugh from the audience, and Nancy found herself blushing.

Feeling herself out on a limb, Nancy explained, "I guess I basically don't think it's great when we treat people as bodies, and not as individuals."

"Hmm." Marcy walked over to a young man on the other side of the aisle. "What do *you* think about that?"

Nancy was struck by the ease with which Marcy handled the opinions of the studio audience. When her theme music came on to signal the end of the show, Marcy signed off to enthusiastic cheers.

"You were all terrific!" Marcy told the audience as she walked among them, greeting them. Several fans asked for autographs, and Marcy busily scrawled her signature for them.

Just then Nancy tugged on George's sleeve. "There's Susan," she said, making her way down the aisle.

Susan was standing between Jack and Brenda Fox, who were all smiles. "Good show, wasn't it?" Brenda was saying.

"Susan, can I speak to you for a minute?" Nancy asked, approaching the small group.

"Sure," Susan said, stepping away from the others.

"Can we look at that photo again?" Nancy asked. "And take a look around Marcy's office?"

Susan led them to the backstage doors. "I heard the show on the loudspeaker," she said. "You sounded terrific."

"You mean you couldn't hear my heart pounding?" Nancy asked with a laugh.

Susan stopped at a small cubicle just outside Marcy's office. "This is my work area," she explained. "I put the photo in my desk." After unlocking a drawer with a key she took from her pocket, Susan pulled out the envelope and handed it to Nancy.

"Jack Cole was in Marcy's office when we were," Nancy said as she dumped the pieces of the photo onto Susan's desk. "But he left when we did, right?"

"Right," Susan said. "And in that next five minutes anyone who works here could have gone in and ripped up the photo. Besides, I don't think Jack could possibly be a suspect. He's been friends with Marcy since they were kids."

Nancy stared at the pieces of the torn photo. "Right now," she said, "everybody's a suspect. Hey, look," she added excitedly, "there's writing on the back of these pieces."

Working quickly, Nancy pieced the photo

together like a jigsaw puzzle. The writing, done in thick magenta marker, began to form words.

"I didn't see that before," George noted.

"I was afraid it might be something like this," Nancy murmured. She stepped aside so the others could read the note.

"Get the message, Marcy? Quit the show—or die!"

Chapter

Three

"WE'D BETTER show this to Marcy right away," Nancy said, shuddering slightly.

"Show me what?" Marcy's voice came from the doorway of the small office. She approached the desk with an anxious expression on her face.

Nancy pointed to the message and frowned. "This." Then she noticed something she hadn't seen the first time. "Check this out," she said. "The marker was running out of ink at the end."

"'Quit or die?'" Marcy read out loud, her voice catching on the last word.

"Marcy," Nancy said, gently touching her arm, "this is a real death threat. I think it's time to contact the police."

"But I hate to do that, Nancy," Marcy said.

"If my producers or the network find out about this, they might think twice about extending my contract. I had a hard time finding sponsors for this show, you know. Not many want to take a chance on a talk show exclusively for young people. Even though my show seems successful—oh, no," she said, interrupting herself. "The *Tribune!* They wanted that photo this afternoon!"

"I'll get the photographer to print another one and send it to the paper," Susan suggested.

"Good thinking, Susan," Marcy said, then added, "Why is this happening to me?"

"Marcy, we really need to talk to you," Nancy said.

"Let's go into my office," the talk show host said quietly. "It's more private there."

Susan had already picked up the phone on her desk to call the photographer. "I'll be in soon," she said. "By the way, Marcy, Vic Molina called and wanted you to call him right back."

"Vic Molina, the television producer?" George asked.

Marcy's face brightened for a second but then collapsed. "I almost forgot he's threatening to sue me," she said, going into her office before Nancy could ask her about the lawsuit.

After replacing the pieces of the photo in the envelope and stuffing the whole thing into her bag, Nancy joined the others. Inside the office,

Marcy picked up the phone and punched in a number. "Excuse me while I handle this," she told Nancy and George.

Nancy listened with one ear as she glanced around the office. Marcy's desk was positioned so that someone could be at the desk but not be seen from the corridor, she noted.

Marcy didn't say much on the phone until she blurted out, "Vic, you're out of control! You're really losing it!" She slammed down the receiver. "You'd think he'd be too busy producing 'Southern Star' and 'Miller's Dream' to bother me, wouldn't you?"

"Those are the two most popular dramas on TV," George remarked.

"The guy's twenty-nine years old, and he's already done more than most fifty-year-olds," Marcy said, her face softening slightly. "I guess you could call him driven."

"Why is he suing you, Marcy?" Nancy asked, settling in a director's chair next to her desk.

"Oh, it's really stupid," Marcy said, running her slender fingers through her hair. "You see, Vic was my boyfriend until six months ago. In fact, he was the one who first suggested I create a talk show. But when I did do it, he got jealous, and we broke up. So I went to the Sterns to produce the show, and, well, Vic went nuts. Now he's claiming the show is half his, and he's suing for fifty percent of the profits!"

"Maybe he's the one who tore up your photo," Nancy suggested. "He sounds pretty angry."

"But, Nancy, how could he have gotten in here? Security is so tight," George said.

"Oh, he could have," Marcy said reluctantly. "'Southern Star' is taped here in the Media Center, up on the fifth floor. Still, it wasn't him, Nancy. I'm sure of it."

"What makes you so sure?" Nancy asked.

Marcy gave Nancy a startled look. "Because I know him," she insisted. "His feelings are hurt now. That's why he's striking out with this stupid lawsuit. But basically he's a good person."

"It sounds like you think a lot of him," Nancy observed, making a mental note to check the sign-in sheets in the lobby to see if Vic had been to the Stern Productions offices that morning.

"We've been through a lot together," Marcy explained. "I know Vic still likes me—deep inside."

"Marcy, can you think of anyone who might have made these threats?" Nancy asked.

Marcy frowned and glanced at her watch. "Well, I know a certain bad-girl singer who's pretty upset with me," she said, aiming a remote control at a TV across the room. "You can see her right now, in fact."

"Bad-girl singer? Do you mean Samantha Savage?" George asked.

"Samantha Savage," came the announcer's voice from the TV as the picture came on. "How bad can a girl get? We're going to find out today on 'Jenny's Place'!"

"Jenny's Place" was a show hosted by the overweight, old-fashioned, but still popular Jenny Dean, one of America's first TV talk show hosts.

"Samantha Savage is here today, everyone! So say hello!" Jenny announced as the camera cut to the sultry singer.

"That black leather skirt of Samantha's couldn't be much tighter," Susan remarked dryly as she came in.

On the screen Samantha had taken a seat and shaken out her flowing bleached blond mane. "It's great to be on a show where you're treated with a little respect, Jenny," Samantha said, pouting.

"Oh? Have you had a bad time on talk shows before, Samantha?" Jenny asked sympathetically.

"Just one, hosted by Marcy Robbins," Samantha said. "That Marcy is a real—oops, I guess I can't say that on television." The TV audience chuckled, more from nervousness, Nancy thought, than agreement.

"Well, why don't you tell us all about it?" Jenny suggested with a syrupy smile.

What followed was a harsh attack on Marcy. "I was on her show two weeks ago, trying to tell her about my new album, *Heartless,* but she was, like, obsessed with talking about my past!"

"Well, what's wrong with that?" Jenny asked. "We're supposed to get to the bottom of things, honey."

Swinging one ankle of her crossed legs, Samantha frowned. "She accused me of being a Girl Scout, Jenny."

At that, the audience let out a big laugh. "She said I never had a date till I was nineteen. In fact, her whole show was about my being a good girl!"

"That *is* a horrible insult, I suppose," Jenny Dean quipped. Then she turned to face the camera. "We're talking with Samantha Savage. How bad can she get? Find out after these messages!"

Marcy clicked off the TV, fuming. "She makes my blood boil!"

"What happened when she was on your show?" Nancy asked, bursting with curiosity.

"I found out the truth about her, that's what happened!" Marcy said hotly. "Her entire bad-girl image is totally bogus. She says she grew up on the streets, poor and abused, and that she's always been a rebel. Well, guess what? She was raised in a rich suburban town and given every advantage, including singing lessons. In grade school she was big in the Girl Scouts, and in high school she was an honor student."

"I guess she wasn't too happy when you revealed all that on TV," George said. "Samantha's built her whole career on her bad-girl image."

"You got it," Marcy agreed. "Now she's saying *I'm* the reason her new album isn't selling the way the others have!" She rolled her eyes. "The worst thing is, I have to see her tonight at a benefit for Lake Shore Children's Hospital."

Susan turned to Nancy and George. "I hope you'll come. It's a celebrity auction."

"That sounds like fun," George said.

Marcy let out a sigh. "To tell the truth, I'm not in the mood for it. I think I'll go home and spend some time with my cat before the benefit. At least he and I get along." Marcy stood up and grabbed a purple satin jacket with the logo of her show on the back, and threw it over her shoulders. "My limo will be at Susan's to pick you up at six forty-five sharp. Be ready, okay?"

"We will," Susan promised. When Marcy was gone, Susan turned to her friends. "We can go now, too. I'm done with my work."

"Not me," Nancy replied. "I want to check

out a few things around here, including the sign-in sheet."

"Okay," Susan replied. "I'll take you and George around, in case anybody gives you a hard time."

"What exactly are we looking for, Nan?" George asked.

Nancy frowned. "Well, for one thing, how about a magenta marker that's low on ink?"

"It *is* an unusual color," Susan said.

Nancy and the girls checked Marcy's office. There were no magenta markers. "You and Susan check the rest of the offices," Nancy instructed George. "Meet me here when you're done."

After they had gone, Nancy figured how much time it would take to enter Marcy's office, write the message, rip up the photo, replace it in the envelope, and sneak away. Not much time at all, Nancy decided. Any Stern employee could have done it.

Then there was Vic Molina. It would have been easy enough for him to get down from the fifth floor, using the fire stairs.

"Four magenta markers between us," George said, holding them up as she and Susan returned.

"But all of them have plenty of ink," Susan added, shaking her head.

"Oh, well," Nancy said. "I guess we'd better get going, huh?"

Susan checked her watch and nodded. The girls headed back down the corridor to the front office, where the receptionist was just preparing to leave.

"Ginger," Susan asked, "did Vic Molina come by today? Or anyone who doesn't work here?"

"Not when I was here," the receptionist told her. "But I took a long lunch and couldn't find anyone to cover for me."

Susan gave the girl a stern look. "You could have called me. Relieving you is part of my job."

Ginger bit her lip. "Sorry, I forgot."

"Ginger," Nancy said, "could you be extra alert about who comes into the offices from now on? It's important."

"Okay," the receptionist agreed, but Nancy wasn't convinced she'd follow through.

"I hope we have better luck with the guard in the lobby," Nancy said as the girls passed through the double doors. Nancy quickly approached the guard and asked, "Would you mind if we take a look at today's sign-in sheets?"

"Fine with me," he said, passing the clipboard to Nancy.

"How many pages should be here?" Nancy asked, riffling through the pages.

"Oh, by this time at least ten," he replied. "This is a busy building."

"Were you ever away?" Nancy asked, handing him back the clipboard.

"Not really," he said. "I might have left for a minute or two to use the men's room."

"There are only four pages here. One from early this morning and three for the past hour and a half," Nancy told him. "Unless I miss my guess, somebody stole the rest."

"Look," said the guard, "I work alone from nine to five, okay? I got to take a short break now and then. I can't—"

Just then Nancy let out a gasp. A cleaning lady had emerged from the Stern offices, pushing a bin of trash in front of her. Before she disappeared through another door marked Staff Only, Nancy noticed something on top of the pile of trash. A magenta marker!

"Where does that door go?" Nancy quickly asked the guard.

"Huh? Oh, to the trash compacter, that's all. Hey! Where are you going?"

Nancy was already halfway across the lobby. She reached the heavy steel door just before it slammed shut. Throwing it open, she raced through. Ahead of her at the far end of the dimly lit room stood the cleaning lady, opening the huge compacter door.

"No, wait!" Nancy screamed.

It was too late. The woman was already tilting her load of trash into the compacter!

Chapter

Four

Fortunately Nancy's scream startled the cleaning lady, causing her to jump just as she tilted the trash. The magenta marker slid off the pile and clattered to the floor at Nancy's feet.

After pulling a tissue from her pocket, Nancy picked it up. "Thanks," she murmured as the cleaning woman watched with a confused expression. "Everything's fine," Nancy assured her, backing away slowly.

"What was that all about?" George asked as Nancy reappeared at the security desk.

Nancy held up the marker to show them. "Let's try it out," she said, and scribbled on a piece of blank paper lying on the guard's desk. The marker was just about dry. "I knew it. People don't throw out markers when they're still working." A grin spread over Nancy's face. "I think this is clue number one."

The girls made their way through the lobby to the front door. After the valet brought Nancy's car around, she and George followed Susan's car out of the downtown area to a neighborhood of town houses and storefronts, where they turned onto a quiet side street and parked. "Like my neighborhood?" Susan asked proudly as she joined them as they unloaded their bags. "It's called Old Town, and it's really cool—lots of art galleries and clubs and antique shops."

They followed Susan into an old brick building, and she led them up to her second-floor apartment. "It isn't big, but it's mine," she said, unlocking the door and ushering them inside.

Susan's decorating skills were what made the place seem cheerful and welcoming, Nancy thought. "I really like these chairs," she told Susan. "Are they antiques?"

Susan laughed. "Nope. I painted them to look old. Come on, I'll show you the rest of the place. We have to get changed, but it's a very short tour."

Off the living room were a small terrace, where Susan stored her bike, a kitchenette, a bathroom, and a tiny bedroom. "This pulls out into a futon bed," Susan said, pointing to the sofa in the living room. "I'll open it up for you later tonight. And that, I think, is the whole tour. So now we can get changed." Susan checked her watch and said, "Uh-oh. Marcy's limo will be here in twenty minutes. Can you be ready in time?"

"No problem," Nancy said with a grin. "George and I are a regular Rapid Deployment Force."

"This place is fabulous," Nancy said as Marcy's limo pulled up to the Harms Wood Country Club, located in posh suburban Evanston, north of the city.

"I love old stone buildings," George said, admiring the facade.

Exquisitely dressed men and women were streaming into the building, and an air of wealth hung over the entire premises.

"Wow," George murmured as a doorman in maroon coat and white gloves pulled a carved oak door open for their group.

"Pretty classy, huh?" Marcy said as she led the way into the large foyer with polished wood paneling and beams that arched gracefully overhead.

Susan reached into her handbag and took out three dark red cards with gold-leaf writing, which she handed to the hostess standing at the entrance to the ballroom, where the auction was to be held.

"You're at table fourteen," the hostess said with a smile.

Stepping into the ballroom, Nancy was taken with the immense crystal chandeliers hanging over each of the fifty or so large round tables.

"I'd better tell the people running this benefit that I'm here," Marcy said, walking away in the direction of the stage, which was curtained in rich wine-colored velvet.

All of Chicago was there, it seemed to Nancy, as she walked past a table with several members of the city's baseball teams.

"I see number fourteen," George said, pointing to a table along the left wall, not far from the stage.

"Drew, Fayne, Ling—that's us," Nancy said, checking the place cards. Then she put her small sequined clutch bag on the table by her setting and walked around the table. "Let's see who else is sitting with us. Mr. and Mrs. Ringer, Mr. Appleby, Ms. Fox—"

"That must be Brenda," Susan said. "She warmed up the audience for Marcy today."

"She seems really nice," George said.

"Brenda's a doll," Susan said. "One of these days I predict she'll be a top producer. She's a hard worker and has everything it takes to succeed."

"Like you," Nancy said, complimenting

Susan. "And here's the last place—Ms. Kristoff."

"Yes?" said a brunette who had just approached the table. She wore a black dress with sequins outlining the scooped neckline.

"Ms. Kristoff!" Susan exclaimed, sounding impressed. "I've always wanted to meet you! My boss, Marcy Robbins, has told me so many nice things about you. I'm Susan Ling, of 'Marcy!' and these are my friends Nancy Drew and George Fayne. We went to high school together."

"How do you do," the woman in black murmured.

"Ms. Kristoff is the executive editor of *Teen Talk,*" Susan explained.

"Please!" the woman said, laughing lightly. "Call me Karen. 'Ms. Kristoff' sounds like someone over forty. I have at least a decade to go before that."

"You must be proud of Marcy," Nancy said.

"I certainly am," the editor gushed. "I picked her out of a bunch of applicants for her very first job. Now she's doing better than I am!"

"You have a great eye for talent," Nancy said.

"That's one way to look at it," Karen said, taking her place.

"Didn't you and Marcy go to high school

together?" Susan asked Karen. "I thought Marcy told me you did."

"She was a freshman when I was a senior," Karen explained. "But I didn't really know her that well back then."

"Marcy said you taught her everything she knows about communicating with people," Susan said.

"Isn't that sweet of her," Karen murmured, and pointed to a vase in the center of the table. It was filled with foot-long placards with large numbers printed on them. Beside the vase was a stack of blank index cards and a crystal container holding several small pencils. "What in the world is all this?"

"Those are the bidding sticks for the auction," Susan explained. "You raise yours to show you want to bid. You write the number of your bid on the cards.

"Hey, there's Brenda," Susan said, turning around as the assistant producer approached the table, smiling.

"Brenda, have you met Karen Kristoff, and my friends Nancy and George?"

"I met Karen at the last Lake Shore Hospital benefit—nice to see you again," Brenda told the editor before turning to Nancy and George. "I noticed you two at today's taping. You both said some good things."

The ballroom was practically full now, and

Nancy sensed from the buzz that the crowd was excited. Onstage Nancy could see Jack Cole adjusting microphone levels.

"I hear they're going to auction the mayor's socks," Brenda said with a laugh. "Who'd ever bid on those?"

"A date with Vic Molina has a lot more appeal to me," Karen Kristoff replied dryly.

"I promised my son I'd bid on the date with Samantha Savage," said Mr. Appleby, a portly man of about fifty who was just sitting down at his place. He nodded to the girls.

Nancy spoke quietly to George and Susan, "I want to keep an eye on Marcy. I'm going to look around backstage."

Nancy made her way to the backstage entrance as the president of the country club took the stage and began to describe the work of the Lake Shore Children's Hospital. Then he introduced Marcy and the fun began.

Marcy was bright and bubbly as she stepped up to the mike. "Okay, folks," she said, "we've got lots of goodies to auction tonight."

Slipping through the little door that led backstage, Nancy moved quickly past Jack Cole, who was standing by the prop table. Nancy waved casually, trying to act as if she belonged there.

Behind the table was a passageway leading to a large room with tall partitions and shelves. The area had been arranged to create individual spaces for changing, Nancy guessed. She weaved quietly around the partitions, looking for any sign of trouble.

Off in a corner, she spotted a shelf with black leather bracelets and metal arm bands. Samantha Savage's tough-girl look came to mind immediately. The expensive-looking red suede jacket emblazoned with *SS* confirmed Nancy's guess that this was where Samantha had changed and made up.

Nancy's gaze fell on a typed letter, which lay on the floor right beneath the jacket. It looked as if it could have fallen out of a pocket. Nancy picked it up and glanced at it.

Sammy, dear, try to keep your feelings about Marcy Robbins under wraps tonight. There's a lot of money in that audience. In fact, this might be a chance to acquire some new fans. Take a bit of advice from your old friend Mort: Stop trying to get Marcy. Remember, she's on top of the heap right now. But sooner or later she'll have to crash. Then you can walk all over her.

Chapter

Five

HER HEART RACING, Nancy thought about pocketing the note but immediately decided against it. The letter was Samantha's personal property.

Nancy had to wonder, though. Exactly how much did Samantha hate Marcy Robbins, and what was the singer capable of doing? And who was Mort?

Nancy had just dropped the note back on the floor where she'd found it when she heard Jack Cole's voice behind her. "Are you lost?" he asked.

"I was told the ladies' room was back here, and I wanted to fix my makeup," Nancy fibbed, reaching for her handbag and pulling out a tube of lipstick. She hoped he hadn't seen her holding the letter. "But this mirror will work fine."

"No one's supposed to be back here but the performers and crew, you know," Jack said suspiciously.

"So, you're part of the crew?" Nancy asked casually.

"Not really. But where Marcy goes, I go. I make sure that things run smoothly for her."

"Really? Well, I'm just leaving, anyway," Nancy said with a quick smile. "Just let me comb my hair a minute. By the way, Susan mentioned that you knew Marcy when you were growing up. Is it true?"

"Yes," Jack answered. "We both grew up in Cicero—out by the racetrack."

"Marcy's such an interesting person," Nancy said, taking a brush to her hair. "What was she like as a kid?"

Jack frowned and rolled his eyes. "Less tense than she is now, that's for sure," he said. "We didn't come from money, but we knew how to have fun."

"How?" Nancy asked.

"Oh, we'd do all sorts of things, wild things," he said with a little smile. "We used to sneak into the racetrack and pet the horses."

"Really? Wasn't it locked up?" Nancy asked.

"Yes," he said, "but we knew ways to get in. Near the stables were a couple of entrances to tunnels that go under Cicero. We went lots of places through those tunnels. It was like our secret."

"There," Nancy said, putting down her brush.

"You'd better get back to the ballroom," Jack said, retreating. "You're missing the whole auction. Come on, I'll show you the way."

They were walking toward the door leading back to the ballroom, when Marcy stomped off-stage, followed by a very angry Vic Molina.

"If you have something to say, say it back here!" Marcy told him over her shoulder. "I don't want to be embarrassed in front of hundreds of people!"

"All right," Vic said, oblivious to Nancy, Jack, and the other stagehands. "I will. Every time a pretty girl bid for that date with me, you totally ignored her!"

"You're being ridiculous," Marcy said. "I just called out the bids I saw. Now, why don't you go out there and have dinner like everyone else?"

"What's the matter? Are you jealous?" The producer's dark eyes were fixed on Marcy's face. "You don't want me, but you don't want anyone else to have me either, is that it?"

"What's the big deal, Vic?" Marcy asked. "This is just a silly auction. Don't you think you're blowing it all out of proportion?"

"I'll show you proportion!" Vic said, grabbing an old stool and smashing it against the wall.

"Vic!" Marcy said, her hands flying to her cheeks.

Nancy stepped back, making sure she was out of the producer's path. What a violent temper, she thought. Glancing over at Jack Cole, she saw his hands ball into fists, ready to join the fight. Luckily, he didn't get the chance.

Vic stormed away. At the ballroom door, he turned back to Marcy and muttered something Nancy couldn't make out.

As soon as he left, Marcy turned to Nancy and Jack. "I have to get back onstage," she said. "It's time to auction off the date with Samantha."

Nancy went into the ballroom as Marcy returned to the stage. But first she noticed Jack staring after Marcy with a hard look on his face.

When the event was over, Marcy's limousine dropped off Susan, Nancy, and George at Susan's house. "I didn't want to say anything in front of Marcy," Susan said as they entered the building, "but I couldn't believe how much Vic Molina bid for that date with Samantha Savage!"

"He sure helped the benefit. It was the

biggest single contribution of the night," George said.

"I loved when the kids from the hospital sang," Nancy said as Susan fished her key from her handbag. "They were so cute."

"Hey, would you two like to go out for some dessert?" Susan asked suddenly.

"How can you think about dessert after that dinner?" George asked.

"True," Susan said, opening the door and leading her friends inside. "I just wanted to show off my neighborhood. It's really the best. But it *is* kind of late."

"And I have a lot of work to do tomorrow," Nancy said, following Susan up the stairs.

Susan unlocked the door of the apartment and flicked on the light so they could enter.

"I'll help open up the bed," Nancy said, walking over to the futon and unhooking one end.

"What's tomorrow's show about, Susan?" George asked, getting her nightgown from her suitcase.

"Parents and teens who don't speak to one another," Susan answered.

"Sounds intense," George said. "What will you be doing?"

"I'll stay with the guests before the show— keep them comfortable, get them soft drinks— stuff like that," Susan explained, sitting on the edge of the futon. Then, changing the subject, she asked, "Who do you think is doing all these awful things to Marcy?"

"Ordinarily, I'd say it would have to be someone at the studio," Nancy said. "But with those missing pages from the security log, I'm not sure. So far, it seems to me that the two people with the most against Marcy are Vic Molina and Samantha Savage. Neither of them works at Stern Productions."

"Speaking of people with something against Marcy," George said, "Karen Kristoff said a lot of nice things about her tonight. But she seemed to be laying it on a little too thick."

"I got the same feeling, George," Susan said. "Hey, I have an idea! *Teen Talk's* offices are right around the corner from the Media Center. My friend Laura is an intern there. Why don't you go over there and look up back issues with information on Vic, Samantha, or Marcy? You could check out Karen Kristoff while you're there."

"Good thinking, Susan," Nancy said, flopping down on the bed. "That's what I call killing three birds with one stone."

After a quick breakfast the next morning, Susan dropped Nancy and George in front of *Teen Talk's* offices. "My friend is Laura Salvo," she told Nancy and George. "Just mention my name and tell her what you need. Oh, and here are your tickets for the show today. The taping is early today. I'll see you later."

"Thanks," Nancy said, sticking the tickets in her bag.

"'Bye, Susan!" George called as the hatchback pulled away.

Nancy and George entered the black granite building through a revolving door. A sign in the lobby told the girls that the magazine's editorial offices were on the fifth floor. The elevator let them off near a metal door emblazoned with the logo of *Teen Talk.* Next to the door of the *Teen Talk* offices was a glassed-in cubicle with a window for talking to the receptionist.

"We're here to see Laura Salvo," Nancy told the young woman seated there, whose hair was pulled back in a thick French braid.

"That's me," the girl replied with a smile.

"Hi, Laura. We're friends of Susan Ling," Nancy said.

"I'll buzz you in," Laura told them without hesitating. After she pressed a button, the door clicked open.

"Hi," Laura said, greeting them at the door. "What can I do for you?"

"Susan thought you could help us out. We're looking for background material on

Samantha Savage, Vic Molina, and Marcy Robbins," Nancy explained. "Back issues, whatever."

"Well, you've come to the right place," Laura said with a laugh. "We have lots of old stories on those three. Wait right here, okay? I'll go check for you."

Nancy and George sat down to wait in two wooden chairs with a small table between them. "This place isn't as nice as I thought it would be," George remarked, looking around.

"I know," Nancy said in agreement. "Maybe the magazine isn't doing very well."

Laura returned a few minutes later. "I'm awfully sorry," she said, looking perplexed, "but any issues with those three seem to be missing."

"What?" George asked, surprised. "How can that be?"

"I wish I knew," Laura said. "It's weird. I'm as baffled as you are. The only thing I can think of is that someone else is checking on the same people. But the magazines should have been signed out."

"Is there anyone you can ask?" Nancy asked.

"I can call Ms. Kristoff. She usually knows everything that goes on around here." Laura sat down and punched in a single digit on the phone. "Hmm, Ms. Kristoff seems to have left her office," she said, hanging up. "I can try her again later. Do you want to wait?"

"No, thanks," Nancy said. "George and I have to get back to the Media Center. Maybe we'll stop by later."

"Do that," Laura said, nodding. "Hopefully, I'll have everything straightened out by then."

"Thanks," Nancy said. She and George got up and left the office.

Outside in the hallway, George checked her wristwatch. "Yikes," she said. "Taping is early today—it starts in ten minutes."

Nancy and George waited impatiently for the elevator, then jogged back to the Media Center. They slid into their seats just in time. "Why do they tape at a different time every day?" Nancy asked. "It's kind of a weird schedule, isn't it?"

"Susan told me why," George replied. "It's because they have to work around the guests' availability. It doesn't much matter because the show airs at five every day. Just as long as it's taped by then, it's okay."

The music came on for the start of the show, and Marcy made her entrance. "We're talking today with people who've stopped talking—to each other," Marcy told the audience, plopping down on the sofa. Across from her sat three teens and three adults. Nancy thought they all looked pretty uncomfortable.

"Meet Trina Myers and her mom, Barbara. And here are Amy Jeffers and her mother, Linda, and Phil Dugan and his dad, Phil senior. These teens and their parents all have something in common. They don't speak to each other! Phil, when was the last time you talked to your dad?"

"Um," the boy said, "it must be a couple of months now."

"It's been over six months, Marcy!" his father corrected angrily.

"Tell us about it," Marcy said to them. "How did it happen?"

What followed were fireworks and tears. The teens and their parents directed their comments to Marcy, almost as if they were communicating through her. It seemed to make it easier for them all to open up.

"Trina claims you never loved her," Marcy told Barbara Myers, who was staring stonily in front of her. "That's a heavy accusation."

"It's totally wrong, too!" Mrs. Myers protested. "Of course, I love her!"

"Hold on to the rest of your thoughts while we break for these messages." Marcy was reading the rolling TelePrompTer that was off to the side and out of camera view. It contained messages for Marcy, such as reminding her of commercial breaks.

All at once, Nancy saw Marcy's face turn white. "Folks, I-I'm terribly sorry," she stammered nervously to the audience. "Please don't panic, but we're all going to have to get out of here right away. I just received a message that there's a bomb planted somewhere in this studio—and it's set to go off any minute!"

Chapter

Six

NANCY SPRANG FROM her seat in the audience and made straight for the talk show host's
side. Nancy read the message on the Tele-
PrompTer: "You didn't quit, so now you'll be
blown away. Bomb goes off at 11:23 sharp."

Pandemonium had broken out in the studio
as the audience pushed for the exits. Nancy,
too, could feel panic rising within her. She
quickly checked her watch. It was 11:16.

"Please, don't panic!" one of the ushers
warned everyone. The look of terror on her
face didn't exactly inspire confidence. Nancy
scanned the mob for the other usher and saw
him speaking into a walkie-talkie. She figured
he was warning security to evacuate the building and call the police.

"George, help everyone get out!" Nancy yelled to her friend. She noticed that the warring parents and teens were helping each other.

Nancy grabbed Marcy's elbow and guided her to one of the wide exits at the back of the studio. There, Nancy recognized the security guard encouraging people to get out quickly.

"Marcy, head for the street!" Nancy yelled, giving her a nudge forward. Across the lobby, she could see George and Brenda Fox holding the doors open to let people exit.

"Do you need help?" Nancy stopped to ask the security guard.

"No, just get out. Please," he urged. "The police will be here any second."

Elevators kept opening, discharging hordes of people from the upper floors, and dozens more poured through the fire-stairs doors. The crunch at the front of the lobby was frightening.

Following the last of the crowd out into the street, Nancy noticed one man strolling outside not far ahead of her. Amid all the panic and fear, his step seemed almost casual. It was Vic Molina! "It's the fifth bomb scare in two years," he was telling the man next to him. "Probably some jerk trying to get attention."

Just then the police arrived. Six or seven cruisers, sirens blazing, cordoned off the street, and two vans marked Bomb Squad pulled up in front of the building, along with an unmarked police car. Five uniformed officers surrounded a short, heavyset man with a walkie-talkie who emerged from this last car. He wore a white button-down shirt that was too small for his expanded belly and a stained navy tie.

"Evacuation is in progress," he said into the device as he strode into the lobby, with his escort clearing the way. "Disposal and I are proceeding to hot spot. Over."

The police had already put up barriers just off the edge of the sidewalk. In front of one barrier, separating her from the anxious crowd and gathering onlookers, was Marcy. She was talking to a silver-haired couple who appeared to be in their fifties. As Nancy edged closer she could hear their conversation.

"You were threatened *before* this morning?" the woman was saying in a shocked tone. "Why didn't you tell Jeff and me immediately? We're your producers, Marcy!"

From what they said, Nancy guessed that the couple were Janet and Jeff Stern, of Stern Productions, the people Marcy most wanted to hide the threats from.

"I'm sorry, Janet. All I can say is that I didn't want to put the show in jeopardy," Marcy said.

"Marcy," Jeff Stern said firmly, his voice rising as he spoke. "A lot of people have a lot of money invested in you and this show, and Janet and I are responsible to them. We have to think about things like lawsuits, security, insurance! Do you realize that if anyone could prove we had reason to anticipate this threat, we could be liable if the Media Center were blown up?"

By then Nancy reached Marcy's side.

"Hi, Nancy," Marcy said weakly as the Sterns turned their attention to the building.

George made her way up to them, too. "Brenda's amazing," she said. "She really knows how to deal with people."

"Has anyone seen Susan?" Nancy asked.

"I'm here," came Susan's voice from behind them. She was with the officer in the civilian clothes. "There's Marcy, Lieutenant," she told him, leading him over to their little group. "Marcy, this is Detective Lieutenant Dunne. He wants to speak with you."

"That's right, Ms. Robbins," said the lieutenant, extending his stubby hand.

Marcy shook it and said, "These are my producers, Janet and Jeff Stern, and these are friends of Susan's, Nancy Drew and George Fayne."

"Nancy Drew, the detective?" the lieutenant asked, raising his eyebrows.

"Yes," Nancy admitted.

"I've read about some of your cases," the lieutenant said. "You're pretty good for a kid." Turning to Marcy, he asked, "How'd you get hooked up with Nancy Drew?"

"Susan suggested I send for her," Marcy explained. "She's been helping me out with a little problem I've been having." Looking around, she asked the lieutenant, "Can we go where it's a little more private?"

Just then two uniformed officers came out of the building, one of them carrying a box, which he brought over to the lieutenant. "Lieutenant Dunne, sir," said the man with the box, "look what we found backstage. It's a phony. One of those party store jobs." Using a handkerchief, he pulled out a round plastic toy bomb with a thick rope sticking out the top and the word *Kapow* written in big letters.

"There was a note, too, sir," said the other officer. He handed it to the lieutenant.

"'Next time it's for real,'" Lieutenant Dunne read aloud. "Done with a laser printer. Oh, well. As soon as you're finished scouring the premises, let these people back inside. Meantime, I'm going into the lobby with these folks."

Lieutenant Dunne led the small group over to the security guard's desk. Sitting on the edge of the desk, he spoke to Marcy. "So what was this problem that caused you to contact a detective?"

"You called in a detective?" Jeff Stern broke in. "Without telling us?"

"Jeff, let the lieutenant ask his questions," Janet Stern told her husband. "We can talk to Marcy later." It was clear to Nancy that the talk would not be friendly.

"I'd been receiving threats," Marcy began. Soon she'd told her whole story up to that point, including reading the message on the TelePrompTer. The lieutenant listened carefully, taking notes. The Sterns listened, too, their faces growing darker by the moment.

"I see," said the lieutenant. "Anything you can add, Nancy?"

"The sign-in sheets for yesterday had several pages missing," Nancy told him. "The guard said he stepped away for only a minute. So, it's not a sure thing that the picture was torn up by someone who works at Stern Productions."

"Well, thank goodness for that," said Janet Stern under her breath.

"Let's have a look at today's sheets, while we're here," said the lieutenant, reaching for the clipboard. After flipping through the first two pages, he stopped short and offered it to Nancy.

Nancy read the name he was pointing to.

"'Adam Bomb.' Hmm. Somebody has a black sense of humor."

Just then the doors to the Stern offices opened, and out came Jack Cole with two officers. "Lieutenant, this is Jack Cole," said one of them. "He led us through the backstage area. He acted very bravely."

"Jack!" Marcy said, putting a hand on his shoulder. "I'm impressed!"

"Aw," Jack said, his face reddening just a bit. "It was nothing. These guys were back there, too."

"Mr. Cole, did you give a statement to the officers?" Lieutenant Dunne asked.

"Yes, I did, Officer," Jack said.

"Okay, then, you can go," Lieutenant Dunne told him. "But I may want to call you later."

"Anything else, Nancy?" Dunne asked her as soon as Jack followed the two officers out of the building.

"I think I may have found the marker that was used to write the threat," she said. "It might have fingerprints on it."

Nancy reached into her bag and handed it to the lieutenant. "We'll check it for prints," he said, pocketing it. "We'll be talking again soon, eh?" Nodding to them all, and taking the clipboard with him, he walked briskly to the front doors. "You can get on with your taping now," he called back to the Sterns. Opening the door, he shouted to his men, "Okay, they can come back in now. The place has been checked out."

As people began reentering the building, the Sterns and Marcy went inside to the offices. Nancy, George, and Susan remained behind. It was obvious that the Sterns wanted to talk to Marcy in private.

When the taping did start up again, half the audience had gone home. By the time it ended, it was almost five o'clock. Nancy, George, and Susan drove back to Old Town in Susan's car and had dinner at a little corner restaurant.

"That was great," George groaned happily as they paid the check. "I'd forgotten how hungry I was."

"Me, too," Susan agreed. "What a day!"

"By the way, I checked out the TelePrompTer before we left the studio," Nancy told them. "Anybody could have written the bomb threat on it. It's all computerized, very user-friendly, and connected to every other computer in the place."

"Not a good day, any way you look at it," Susan said, shaking her head. "And Marcy was pretty shaken up by her talk with the Sterns."

"I thought the show went fantastically well, though," George said. "Maybe it was *because* of what happened, but the guests seemed to be a lot more comfortable afterward."

"Nothing like a little bomb threat to put things in perspective, I guess," Susan said as they finished paying the cashier and walked out the door.

Nancy shook her head. "I'm worried," she confessed as they walked toward Susan's building. "Up to now, it's only been threats. But these things tend to escalate."

"The Sterns were awfully upset with Marcy," Susan said as they entered her building. "I guess Marcy should have told the producers there was a problem when it first came up."

"The threats might have turned out to be nothing more than pranks. It was a hard decision for Marcy to make," Nancy said.

"I guess so." Susan unlocked her door and reached in to flick on the lights. "Let's hope Janet Stern is understand—"

Susan's comment was cut short by a gasp. "What happened here?" she said, stepping inside the apartment.

"Oh, no!" George said from behind Susan. "There's broken glass everywhere!"

A quick peek showed Nancy that only a few jagged pieces remained in the frame of the hall mirror. The rest of the mirror lay in shards on the floor.

"Look! This has your name on it, Nancy," Susan said breathlessly, reaching down to pick up an envelope.

Nancy took the envelope, tore it open, and yanked out a piece of paper. What she read made her feel as though she'd been punched in the stomach.

"Nancy Drew, get out of town or your face will look like this mirror!"

Chapter

Seven

NANCY PASSED the threatening note to George and Susan. "This is pretty ugly," she said, "but I'm going to look at it in a positive way. Even if we don't think that we're getting anywhere, the culprit must—he or she is definitely feeling threatened by us."

"Or maybe *they* are feeling threatened," George added.

"Gosh, I never thought of that," Susan said, giving the note back to Nancy. "There could be more than one person after Marcy—and now they're after you, Nancy."

"It sure looks that way," Nancy said, and placed the note on the hall table as George went to get a dustpan and broom. "How do they know about me?" Nancy said, frowning.

"How do they know where I'm staying? You didn't tell anyone that we were coming to investigate, did you, Susan?"

The expression on Susan's pretty face was all the answer Nancy needed. "The day that Marcy got the first threat, I was very upset," she confessed. "I started talking about what happened to Brenda Fox. I think Dee, the hairdresser, was there, too. I said I knew someone who might be able to help, and I'm pretty sure I said your name, too. Oh, how could I have been so stupid?"

"Forget about it," Nancy reassured Susan. "You didn't know anything like this would happen." Privately, Nancy made a mental note to question Dee and Brenda the next chance she got.

When the girls had finished cleaning up, Nancy went to the front door and examined the lock. "This door looks fine," she said. "No forced entry here."

"Maybe the culprit used a key to get in," George said.

"I have only two keys," Susan told her. "I have one, and the spare I gave to George."

"It's in my pocket," George said, pressing her hand against her hip to make sure.

"Let's assume they got in another way then," Nancy suggested, walking through the living room to the double sliding doors that led out to the terrace.

"The door is open a crack!" George exclaimed, following Nancy.

"Watch for prints!" Nancy cautioned before George could touch the handle.

"Right," George agreed. She headed into the kitchen and emerged a moment later with a dish towel covering her hands.

"Susan, why don't you look around to see if anything else has been disturbed," Nancy suggested.

"Okay," Susan said.

George slid the door open, and Nancy followed her out to the terrace.

"This door is all scratched and chipped," Nancy observed, pointing to the outside edge. "Susan's going to need a new lock."

"And the terrace isn't so high that someone with a little ingenuity couldn't have gotten up to it," George said.

"Must have been quite an athlete, though, to climb up that bush and then twist over to reach for the terrace railing." Nancy figured that the chances of anyone witnessing the person were slim since the terrace opened onto a courtyard.

Susan rapped on the glass just then. She pointed to a scrap of blue paper on the terrace.

Nancy bent down and picked it up. "It's got a phone number on it," she said, "written in pencil."

"Well, let's call it," George suggested.

"Nothing else has been touched," Susan told

the girls when they stepped back into the apartment. "Is that paper anything important?"

Nancy showed it to Susan. "It has a phone number on it." Nancy pressed in the numbers. "It's ringing."

"Hello!" came a recording on the other end, "You got Pepe's Garage. Come to Pepe's where stars park their cars. We're closed now until six A.M. But leave a message, after the beep. *Beeeeep—*"

"We'll have to look up the address," Nancy murmured as she hung up.

The next morning the girls took Nancy's Mustang to the Media Center and went straight in to Stern Productions.

Marcy was already in her office. "I don't know who's going to show up for the show today after that bomb scare," she said. "Look at all these negative headlines!" As she spoke, she pushed a pile of newspapers across her desk for Nancy and the girls to read. The headlines said things like "'Teen Talk' Bombs!" "Talk About Trouble!" and "Mad Bomber Stalks Talk Show Star!"

Closing Marcy's office door for privacy, Nancy told her about the break-in at Susan's apartment.

"That's horrible! You've got to tell Lieutenant Dunne right away," Marcy insisted.

"That's what I'm planning to do." Nancy dialed the number of police headquarters, but she had to leave a message for Lieutenant Dunne, who was out.

"I think he said he'll come by the studio later," Marcy told them. "He wants to do some more looking around and ask some more questions."

"What's today's topic?" George asked Marcy and Susan.

"We're having an open call-in show today. That means we'll talk about whatever our callers want," Marcy told her. "Dr. Helen is going to be here, answering calls."

"Dr. Helen is my absolute favorite," George said. "I read her book, *Being Your Best,* and loved it."

"Everybody loves Dr. Helen," Marcy agreed. "She's incredibly understanding."

"America's best-loved psychologist," Nancy added, parroting the phrase most often used about the famous doctor.

"Yikes, I'm late for hair and makeup," Marcy said, checking her watch.

"Knock, knock." Jack Cole's voice came from the other side of the door just as Marcy was about to open it. "Brenda asked me to tell you that taping has been delayed," he said, peeking inside. "Dr. Helen had an emergency, and she can't get here until one-thirty."

"Oh, no," Marcy said. "That's going to cost

the Sterns money. And what are we going to do with the audience? They'll have to hang around for hours!"

"I have an idea," Susan suggested. "I can arrange for them to have a tour of the center, and then order in box lunches. I can even use the time to drum up a fuller house."

"Susan, you're a genius," Marcy said, beaming at her.

"I'll go tell Janet," Jack said, nodding at the girls.

When Jack left, Nancy turned to Marcy and Susan. "George and I will see you at the taping," she said, heading for the door.

"Where are you going?" Susan called after them.

"Where the stars park their cars," Nancy quipped, as she and George strode down the hallway. "Pepe's, here we come."

Nancy and George retrieved the Mustang, but it hardly turned out to be necessary. In less than five minutes they pulled up across the street from Pepe's Garage.

"Well, let's go in," Nancy said, opening the car door and getting out.

Walking with George into the freshly painted, well-maintained garage, Nancy noticed that the small inner glass booth was plastered with publicity photos of models, dancers, and actors. Most were signed "To Pepe—With Love." Several photos showed a heavyset man wearing one gold earring and a wide grin, his arm flung around the shoulder of various celebrities.

"Hey, George," Nancy said. "Check out the fifth picture from the left—"

"That's Samantha Savage before she bleached her hair blond!" George exclaimed.

"Hello, girls, something I can do for you?" The chubby man Nancy assumed to be Pepe was walking toward them. "Some gallery, huh? I got even more at home."

"There sure are a lot," Nancy said.

"Pepe knows everybody. I got them all," the garage owner bragged. "I got dancers, I got singers, actors, models, even big-time producers. Everybody parks their car with Pepe."

"Producers? Producers like Vic Molina?" Nancy asked, acting impressed.

Pepe grinned and nodded. He pulled a snapshot from his pocket and showed it to the girls. He and Vic Molina were standing in front of a red sports car. "This is two days ago," Pepe said. "Mr. Molina keeps all his cars at Pepe's."

"Well, I need a garage for my car," Nancy fibbed. "The last place I used, the spaces were so tiny it got nicked and scraped constantly. Any chance we can check out the facilities?"

"Please, help yourself," Pepe said, moving his arms expansively. "We go down three levels. All nice and clean. And plenty of room for every car."

"Great," Nancy said cheerfully. She and George started walking down the railed sidewalk next to where the cars were driven. Nancy wasn't sure what she was looking for, but that piece of paper could be a lead.

"Do you think there's any connection between Samantha and the break-in at Susan's apartment, Nan?" George asked. "I mean, her picture is here, right?"

"For that matter, so is Vic Molina's," Nancy pointed out. "Anyhow, I find it hard to believe that Samantha Savage would break into a second-floor apartment." Then, suddenly, from the other side of the pillar just ahead of them, Nancy heard voices. She and George froze. The voices were those of Vic Molina and Samantha Savage!

"She doesn't care who she hurts," Samantha was saying bitterly. "All she cares about is herself."

"Don't let it upset you," Vic replied. "The show is finished."

"What about Marcy?" Samantha hissed. "I want her out of the picture, Vic. Know what I mean?"

George edged a little closer, but as she did so she kicked a soda can. The noise wasn't exactly deafening, but it was loud enough.

The producer and star stopped talking. In the silence, George shot Nancy a panicked, apologetic look. Nancy put a hand out to comfort her friend but jerked it back when Vic came storming around the pillar. Angrily, he advanced on Nancy and George, shouting, "Hey! Look at this, Samantha, somebody's spying on us!"

Chapter

Eight

"Spying?" Nancy said as indignantly as she could. "Us?" She tried to return the producer's hard stare.

"How long have you been hiding here?" Molina demanded, looking from Nancy to George and back again. "And don't try to tell me you were going to your car. I'd have heard you moving around."

Samantha came up behind Vic, her eyes flashing fire. "Who are these girls? Do you know them?" she asked him.

"They were at the benefit," Vic answered, sourly. "I believe they're friends of Marcy's."

"*Fans* of Marcy Robbins, Mr. Molina," Nancy corrected him, thinking fast. "And fans of *yours,* too. Your show, 'Southern Star,' has changed my life! It's the greatest show I ever saw!"

"And you're the best singer in the world, Samantha," George added, playing along. "Your new CD, *Heartless*—it's totally awesome!"

At this, Samantha's face lost its hard edge. "Thanks," she told George.

"That's why we came down here," Nancy went on. "To try to get autographs. Oh, please, could you?" Reaching into her pocket, she brought out the pad she always carried to take notes on.

Vic didn't know whether to believe Nancy and George or not. "I don't like people sneaking up on me," he muttered angrily. "And we don't give autographs!" Taking Samantha's arm, he guided her down to his car. With a slamming of doors and a screech of tires, Molina backed out of his spot and sped from the lot.

"Sorry, Nan," George said, shaking her head. "I really goofed. I should have seen that soda can."

"Come on, don't be so hard on yourself," Nancy said comfortingly. "At least we learned something. Vic and Samantha obviously have it in for Marcy. But if either one of them knew I was a detective, they did a good job hiding it."

"They were having a secret meeting here!" George said, her voice rising with excitement. "Maybe he and Samantha are working together to get Marcy. Maybe we just broke the case!"

"I wish I agreed, George," Nancy told her friend. "But we can't prove a thing against Vic Molina, Samantha Savage, or anybody else. We can't prove they were anywhere near the studio when Marcy's photo was ripped or when the phony bomb was planted."

"True," George said, sounding discouraged now.

"We'll just have to keep on working," Nancy said with determination.

After a quick lunch at a coffee shop, Nancy and George drove back to the Media Center and parked in the underground garage. Upstairs in the Stern offices, they found Susan in the corridor going to her cubicle.

"Nancy! George!" she cried when she saw them. "Guess what?" she said with a smile. "The crowd not only stayed around, it grew! The Sterns think the bomb threat could send our ratings through the roof."

"Life sure is strange," George said.

"Especially life in TV," Susan joked.

"Look who's here," Nancy said as Lieutenant Dunne appeared at the end of the hall. Beside him was a short, dark-skinned man dressed in a blue shirt and black pants. "Hi, Lieutenant Dunne," Nancy called.

"Oh, hi, everyone," he said, walking up to the three girls. "Meet Eddie McCormack. He's setting up phone taps. If any more phone threats come in, we can trace the call and get the voice on tape. Come on, Eddie, let's check with the front switchboard."

"Lieutenant Dunne," Nancy said, stopping him. "Can I talk to you for a second?"

"If it's about that marker, I don't know a thing yet," he said. "The lab is a little backed up. I should hear something by tomorrow morning."

"It's not about that," Nancy explained.

The lieutenant sighed a little impatiently and leaned against the wall.

"There was a break-in at Susan's apartment last night, the place where George and I are staying."

Lieutenant Dunne became instantly alert. "What did they take? Why didn't you call right away?"

"It's not what they took," Nancy said. "It's what they left—a broken mirror and a note warning me off the case."

"Shook you up a little, huh?" he said.

Nancy smiled. "Not exactly, but you might want to send someone over there to dust for prints. If there are any, they'd be on the terrace door. You can get the key from George or Susan."

"Yeah, well, I might just do that," the lieutenant replied, taking out his notepad and making a note. Then he stood up straight and stuck his pen behind his ear. "I guess I don't have to tell you to be careful. I mean, a famous detective like you."

There was a touch of humor in his voice, which Nancy noted.

"Just keep in touch, you hear?" Then he headed off in the direction of the switchboard.

"Ten minutes to show time," Susan said from behind Nancy. "Here are your tickets, guys. Enjoy Dr. Helen."

Nancy and George headed toward the studio, and on the way saw Brenda and Dee talking in one of the offices. Nancy poked her head in. "Excuse me, you two," she said apologetically. "I know it's almost show time, but I have a couple of important questions. Do you have a second?"

Brenda checked her watch. "A second," she said tentatively, "but that's about it."

"I understand Susan told you about me before I got here. Did either of you repeat that information to anybody?"

Brenda and Dee shared a guilty glance. "Well, we talked about it with Ginger, actually. You know how hard it is to keep a secret," Brenda said.

"And I think I told Midge," Dee confessed. "I knew I shouldn't tell her, but somehow she wormed it out of me."

"Thanks for your time," Nancy said. "And one other thing, do either of you know anyone in Stern Productions who might have something against Marcy?"

Brenda shook her head. "Lieutenant Dunne asked me the same thing yesterday afternoon. But, no—everyone here is nuts about Marcy."

"That's right," Dee agreed. "We all love her to pieces."

"Even Jack Cole?" Nancy prodded.

"Especially Jack," Dee said with a little laugh. "He's got a crush on her, if you ask me. They go way back. It's like he's appointed himself her watchdog or something. Always looking out for her. Why would he do anything to hurt her?"

"Well, the other day, he seemed a little annoyed with her," Nancy said. "He called her Queen Marcy, for one thing."

"Oh, that's just his sense of humor," Brenda explained. "He's a little strange that way. But he cares about her a lot."

"Well, thanks," Nancy told them. "I don't want to keep you any longer. Have a great show. Come on, George." With a wave, Nancy led George into the studio where they found their way to their seats in the packed house. Everyone was buzzing about the bomb threat.

As the show's music faded, Marcy Robbins stepped into the spotlight, wearing a loose-fitting floral-print dress with a scoop neck.

"Thanks, everyone," she said, answering the enthusiastic applause that flooded the studio. "Welcome to 'Marcy!'—that's me!" She flopped down on the edge of one of the blue sofas and talked to the audience in a more personal way. "Hey, do you have a problem with your mom, dad, boyfriend, or girlfriend? I guess we all have problems of one sort or another. Today we have someone here who can help solve them all! After the break we'll meet Dr. Helen Cavallacci—better known to you as Dr. Helen!"

Wild cheers exploded in the audience, and the show went to its first commercial break. When it came back on, Marcy introduced her guest.

"She's a lot younger looking in person," George whispered as the famous psychologist stepped on the stage and took a seat on the sofa. Her snowy hair fell in soft curls around her smiling face, and her bright blue eyes seemed to twinkle merrily.

"What a nice welcome," she said appreciatively.

"Practically everybody in the world looks to you for advice, Dr. Helen," Marcy said as her guest sat down. "Everyone reads your newspaper column, too—princes, corporate leaders, schoolteachers, and plumbers. Why do you think that is? And how did it all begin?"

"Oh, stop flattering me. It isn't necessary," Dr. Helen said in her down-to-earth, grandmotherly way. She brushed aside Marcy's compliments with a wave of her hand. "I'm just an old lady who's been around a little, that's all."

The audience broke out in laughter at the psychologist's folksy modesty.

"Wait a minute," Marcy challenged. "Isn't it true that you've been getting calls from the White House lately?"

"How did you know?" the psychologist asked, surprised.

"Hey, that's what I do for a living. Find things out," Marcy quipped.

"Well, it's true, Marcy," Dr. Helen admitted. "I get calls from the President and his family from time to time. Everyone thinks people in high positions are invulnerable, but they have little personal problems, too. Everybody does."

"Could you share some of the questions someone in power might have for you?" Marcy asked.

"I can't reveal my clients' secrets," Dr. Helen said, laughing off the request. "That's confidential. They'd never call me again if I did!"

Nancy joined the rest of the audience, laugh-

ing at the candid remark. "Well, there you
have it, folks," Marcy told the audience.
"She's the secret consultant to the powers-
that-be, and today she's here to talk to *you!*
Just call 1-312-555-TALK to talk to Dr. Helen.
Are you ready to take the first call, Dr. Helen?"

"Fire away," the psychologist said, smoothing out her deep green skirt.

"Okay, then, let's go to our first caller,"
Marcy said, pressing a button on a rectangular
box atop the coffee table in front of her. "This
is Marcy. You're on the air, talking to Dr.
Helen."

Over the sound system came the voice of an
extremely timid-sounding girl. "Dr. Helen, I
have a boyfriend who is totally into watching
sports on TV. That's all he ever wants to do,
and I find it very boring. But he says if I really
like him, I'll watch with him. What should I
do?"

George gave Nancy a nudge and whispered,
"Sounds like my kind of guy." Nancy giggled.
George was a big sports fan.

"I think you should find a boyfriend who
likes to do the things you like to do," Dr. Helen
answered the caller. "I'm with you, he sounds
very boring. Either tell him to limit his TV
viewing or go find someone else!"

The next caller was the mother of a teenage
girl. "My fifteen-year-old daughter doesn't

think that she should have a curfew on week-ends. She says having a curfew means I don't trust her."

"Of course you don't trust her," the psychologist said. "No parent should trust a teenager! Right?"

The way she said it made Nancy, George, and the rest of the audience laugh again. But then the psychologist turned more serious. "No, really, parents and children need to be able to trust each other, but they've got to *earn* one another's trust. I believe the curfew is really in your daughter's best interests. Once she understands that it's for her protection I think she'll accept the idea of it more easily. If she doesn't, tell her to write to me!"

Marcy smiled and went on to the next call. "This is Marcy," she said, "and you're talking to Dr. Helen. Go ahead, please."

This time the voice that came through the sound system sent a cold chill up Nancy's spine. "Dr. Helen," it said in a weird electron-ically distorted pitch, "how do you explain a person who won't take a warning?"

"What kind of warning are you talking about?" the psychologist asked.

"A warning to quit hosting a certain TV show," the weird voice said. Nancy bit her lip and listened even harder. Marcy's face had turned white, she noticed.

"Please, stop being so coy," Dr. Helen said, sounding annoyed. "Why don't you just say what you called to say."

"All right, then. I'm not the person who set the phony bomb—but I know who did. Let this be a warning to you, Marcy. The person who did it means business and is running out of patience. Quit this show now—*today,* Marcy—or you're dead!"

Chapter

Nine

Wₑ'ₗₗ BE RIGHT BACK after these messages," Marcy said as a fearful stir swept through the studio. She fell back against the sofa, stunned. The murmur from the audience grew louder.

From behind the set, Lieutenant Dunne appeared, asking Dr. Helen to keep the caller on the line.

Brenda Fox, who was sitting on a stool off the set but in plain view of the audience, got to her feet instantly. "Folks, what we need now is quiet," she told the crowd.

"Caller? Are you still there?" Dr. Helen asked, her voice firm and calm.

"Yes," the electronically altered voice replied. "I'm still here."

Nancy gripped George's arm tightly. "I hope

the police will be able to make a trace," she said.

"Nancy, do you recognize the voice?" George asked.

"I can't even tell if it's a man or a woman," Nancy said in frustration.

"You're very angry, aren't you? Obviously you want to talk about it, or you wouldn't have called today," the psychologist persisted. "I want to understand where your anger is coming from."

"Marcy Robbins steps all over people. She doesn't care who she hurts."

At those words, Marcy leaned forward, shaking her head, dumbfounded.

"Marcy stepped all over *you?*" Dr. Helen asked, gently challenging the caller. "And now you want to get even? Is that it?"

"Yes, but like I said, I'm not the one she should be scared of," the voice replied, its strange pitch rising.

"What you are saying is very serious," Dr. Helen said. "I can tell you're carrying around a heavy load. Won't you feel better if you reveal yourself and this other person? Why should you burden yourself with all this?"

"I've said what I have to say," the voice shouted now. "You can't make me say more."

With that the caller banged the receiver down. Lieutenant Dunne poked his head back in and nodded gratefully to Dr. Helen. Marcy sat up. "It was the same person who left me the message," she said to Lieutenant Dunne.

"We'll start taping again as soon as you're ready, Marcy," Nancy heard Brenda say to the host. "Take your time, but remember, we do have other callers waiting on the lines." Then she turned to the audience. "Thanks for your cooperation, folks. Let's not let that call ruin our show."

Nancy tugged on George's sleeve and stood up. "Let's go find Lieutenant Dunne," she said, passing to the aisle with George close behind.

Nancy and George made their way behind the set to where the studio connected with the Stern offices. Because of the police presence, Nancy guessed, the door was open. They found the lieutenant and a couple of his staff in Mr. Stern's office, which now looked like a police command center.

Nancy and George were about to step inside when they heard the lieutenant say, "The call came from the lobby of a building right next door."

He wasted no time hurrying out the door. "Girls!" he said, surprised to see them in the corridor.

"We heard what you said," Nancy told him as he passed by her. "Can I come?"

"Sure," he said, without stopping. "I know you'll take care of yourself."

"Stay here and keep an eye on things, George," Nancy said, hurrying after him. "I'll be right back."

"It's probably too late, but you never know," the lieutenant said over his shoulder as they passed through the lobby to the street exit.

Threading past pedestrians on the busy sidewalk, they entered the lobby next door. There they quickly spotted a bank of phones across from a newspaper and candy stand. Nancy was disappointed to see that all the phones were free. They had arrived too late.

"Excuse me," the lieutenant said to the dark-skinned man stacking candy under the newsstand. "Did you see anyone at any of those phones a few minutes ago?"

"Sorry," the man answered. "I didn't pay attention."

"I saw someone," the woman behind the counter answered. She, too, had dark skin and long smooth black hair. The Indian sari she wore was a deep rose color. "At the last phone."

"Yes?" the lieutenant asked eagerly. "Man or woman?"

"It was a woman, but I didn't see her face," the concessionaire told him. "She wore a paisley scarf, very beautiful, black and red, with gold thread woven in."

"Was she tall, short, fat, thin?" The lieutenant pressed for more description.

The woman looked confused. "Medium, I guess. I really didn't pay much attention," she said with a regretful shrug. "She made a call, and then she was gone."

"A black and red scarf with gold thread, huh?" Lieutenant Dunne repeated.

"Yes, she covered her head with it," the woman said.

"Which way did she go when she left?" Nancy asked.

"Let's see," the woman said, obviously trying to remember. "That way, I think." She pointed to the far side of the phone bank, where the building's service entrance was.

"'Employees Only,'" the lieutenant read the words printed on the door. "'All Others— Keep Out.'" He turned to Nancy and reached for the doorknob. "Come on, Nancy."

"Hey! No one's allowed in there!" came a shout. Turning, Nancy saw the building's uniformed security man approaching rapidly.

Reaching into his jacket pocket, Lieutenant Dunne pulled out a bronze badge. "Chicago PD," he said, flashing it.

"What's going on?" the security man asked, frowning.

"Police business," the lieutenant said. "Did you happen to notice anyone on those phones in the last five minutes?"

"I was out front," the guard replied.

"Where does this door lead?" Nancy asked him.

"Out back to the parking lot. See for yourself." With that he opened the door leading to a ten-foot-long corridor ending in a freight exit. The door was slightly ajar, revealing a slice of the lot behind the building.

"There's how she got away," Nancy said, frustrated.

"Don't let anybody near that last phone," the lieutenant told the guard. "I'm going to send someone to check it for prints. But first, I want to have a quick look out back."

After following the lieutenant down the short corridor, Nancy stepped outside. Next to the door were three large trash and recycling containers, which she peered into.

"Nothing in there," the lieutenant said.

But a glint of gold from behind one of the containers caught Nancy's eye. "Fantastic!" she said, reaching down and pulling up the paisley scarf. "Somebody was in a hurry, I guess."

"Good work, Nancy!" the lieutenant said, taking the scarf from her and checking out the label. "'One hundred percent rayon. Cold wash only,'" he read. "We'll run a check on this."

Nancy looked across the parking lot at the black granite building across the way. It sent a shock of recognition through her. It was the building that housed the offices of *Teen Talk*. "I never heard from Laura," she murmured softly.

"What's that, Nancy?" the lieutenant asked.

"That building is where I was trying to get some background information on Marcy, Vic Molina, and Samantha Savage," she said.

"Yeah, I heard about those two from Marcy yesterday," the lieutenant said. "We've checked into them, but they seem to be okay. I don't think either of them could have sneaked into the Stern offices without being recognized."

"But remember, Lieutenant," Nancy reminded him, "the caller today said there was somebody else involved. Maybe Vic or Samantha is working with someone at Stern Productions."

"You have a lot of fancy theories, Nancy," the lieutenant said. "You check them out, okay? I've got a lot of cases I'm working on at the moment. Now if you'll excuse me," he said, turning to go back into the building, "I've got to call headquarters to send a fingerprint guy over here."

Nancy ran across the parking lot to go to see Laura at the offices of *Teen Talk*. There was a different receptionist behind the glass partition.

"I'm looking for Laura Salvo," Nancy said.

"Oh," said the receptionist, taking off her glasses and staring at Nancy. "Laura's no longer here."

"What happened to her?" Nancy couldn't hide her surprise.

"Ms. Kristoff let her go. It was kind of sudden," the girl said. "I'm new here, so I really couldn't tell you."

"I see." Nancy checked her watch. "Thank you. Thank you very much." She headed straight back to the Media Center.

There George was waiting for her by Ginger's desk. "Big news, Nancy," George said, her face tight with worry. "Taping of 'Marcy!' has been postponed until further notice."

"Oh, no," Nancy said. "Poor Marcy. How is she taking it?"

"She's talking to the Sterns right now," George told her. "Susan's in on the meeting, too. Apparently, it was something about the show's insurance being canceled. The company said that all the threats were making it too much of a risk. By the way, Susan just handed me this. She said somebody left it in her box, but it has your name on it."

Nancy quickly opened the envelope and pulled out a sheet of notepaper.

Nancy—I couldn't get those files for you, but I found out something you should know. Meet me at 1331 Western Avenue this afternoon. Go up the stairs. I'll be waiting, and I'll explain everything. It's important that you come alone. Thanks. Laura Salvo.

Nancy handed the note to George. "I've got to follow this up."

"I'll come with you," George said after reading the note.

Nancy shook her head. "It says *alone,* George. But I'll tell you what. If you don't hear from me within an hour, come after me, okay? Here are my car keys—I'll cab it."

"Are you sure, Nan?" George asked. "I smell a rat."

"You're not the only one," Nancy agreed. "I was just over at *Teen Talk.* Laura's been fired."

"Do you think it was because of us?" George asked.

"I don't know," Nancy said, frowning. "I guess I'll find out from Laura. But in any case, I do think we ought to have a little chat with Karen Kristoff. She might be able to fill in some holes."

Saying goodbye to George and Ginger, Nancy went back out into the street and hailed a cab. She gave the cabbie the address and leaned back against the seat to think.

The case was confusing, and Nancy's best clues, like the marker and the scarf, were with the police. Two things Nancy was almost sure of: the caller had been telling the truth on that day's show—there was another person involved, and the other person worked at Stern Productions.

Although the sign-in sheets had been stolen and a phony name written in, Nancy decided that only a Stern insider would have had the knowledge to get about quickly backstage, known how to fool with the TelePrompTer, and been able to come in and out without anyone noticing.

As the cab drove on, the neighborhoods grew shabbier and shabbier, and more and more industrial. This part of Western Avenue was full of old warehouses, auto body repair shops, and corner convenience stores. The address 1331 Western was a large, two-story wooden building, with bars on the windows and a sign in front that said America Plus Stage Scenery. After paying the cabbie, Nancy got out and went over to the heavy front door.

She knocked, and after a minute, when nobody answered, she tried the handle. The door was unlocked. Stepping inside, Nancy found herself in a little vestibule, with a door on the left, which Nancy assumed went to the first-floor warehouse, and a flight of steps on the right.

Nancy remembered that the note had told her to go upstairs. She did so, slowly, her ears alert to any stray noise she might hear. But the building was utterly silent. Too silent.

At the top of the stairs Nancy stopped and looked around. There were several empty rooms that opened on to an empty hallway. No furniture anywhere. The windows were all barred, too. "Laura?" Nancy called out. There was no response. Again she said, "Laura? Are you there? It's me—Nancy Drew."

Then she heard a door opening downstairs. As Nancy turned to go back down, she heard a liquid being poured and began to smell something that reminded her of gasoline. "Laura?" she called out again as she started down. "What's going—?"

Her words were cut off as a door was slammed and a huge fireball burst up from the bottom of the stairs. Someone had set the building on fire!

Chapter

Ten

NANCY HASTILY retreated back up the stairs as thick smoke rose after her. She ran along the corridor, checking each room. Every window was locked and fastened with vertical iron bars.

Soon she was coughing from the choking smoke, which was getting thicker by the moment. How could she have been so foolish as to walk into a trap! George wouldn't be coming after her for another half hour at least!

Holding a handkerchief over her nose to filter out the smoke, Nancy searched frantically for any means of escape. Finally, in one of the side offices, she saw an ancient and dusty air conditioner fitted into the wall. Racing to it, she gave it a swift karate kick, and to her great relief, it budged. After three or four more kicks, the old machine caved in a bit, creating a small hole for Nancy to breathe through. She gratefully took a few hurried gulps of air. Around her, the heat of the fire was rising. Horrified, Nancy peered into the hall and saw flames dancing across the floorboards at the top of the steps.

Unless she could knock the air conditioner completely out, she was doomed and she knew it. Flames were even licking at the doorway of the little office she was in. Her only exit was blocked!

"Nancy!" Over the roar of the flames, Nancy heard George's voice from outside—probably from the front of the building. "Nancy, are you in there?"

"Up here, George!" Nancy screamed through the tiny hole. "By an air conditioner!" Below her, in what Nancy assumed to be an alley, she heard footsteps approaching and stop right below her.

"George, did you come in my car?" Nancy asked.

"Yes!" George called up to her.

"Can you back it up under this window?" Nancy asked.

"I think so."

"Good. There's a rope in the trunk. If you can loop it around the air-conditioner supports, you might be able to drive the car forward and yank it free!"

"Got it!" George yelled. In a minute Nancy heard a car backing into the alleyway. Behind her, flames were inching across the room. The smoke was making everything dark. Nancy felt as if she might pass out. She would have if it hadn't been for the small hole letting air in.

Suddenly the air conditioner was jerked, and Nancy knew that George and the car were working the supports loose. Just as the heat from the flames grew unbearable, there was the screeching of tearing metal and the air conditioner fell out, landing hard with a crash.

In no time Nancy was through the hole, and holding on to the ledge, she lowered herself to the ground. Gulping fresh air, she looked down. The alley was about seven feet below her feet. Nancy braced herself and let go.

She landed hard. At the impact, her lungs hurt—but she was alive! George put an arm around Nancy and helped her up. Together they staggered back to the car. "I'm okay, I really am," Nancy gasped. "Now go call the fire department. I'll wait here."

George took off, and Nancy climbed into the car. She backed it a safe distance away from the burning building, which was now fully engulfed in flame. One by one, the windows exploded, and flames shot out like grasping fingers.

Nancy slumped over the wheel. "That caller

was right—somebody really means business," she whispered, still trying to steady herself. "And something tells me it wasn't Laura Salvo."

Just then George came back. "Are you okay?" she asked, opening the driver's side door. "You look horrible."

"I feel wonderful," Nancy rasped, coughing a couple of more times as she slid across the seat so George could get in. "How did you get here so fast?"

George giggled and gave her friend a quick, tight hug. "I got to thinking after you left," she told Nancy. "I didn't know if Laura Salvo even knew your last name. I decided I had to come after you."

"Thanks," Nancy said with a smile. "Anytime you want to use your head to save my life, I give you permission."

The fire crew arrived moments later. "Smoke inhalation can be serious. You were lucky," one fire fighter told her as Nancy took a dozen deep breaths from the portable oxygen supply they carried. "In fact, I recommend you get to a hospital to have your carbon monoxide level checked."

"Can't," Nancy said. "The person who set this fire is out there somewhere, and I've got to stop him—or her."

"Are you sure you don't want to go to a

hospital?" George asked when they got back in Nancy's car.

Nancy leaned back in the passenger seat. "No way, George."

"Well, where to?" George asked, starting the engine.

"Let's go to Susan's place," Nancy said. "I want to call Lieutenant Dunne right away. I want to talk to Susan about the show being canceled, and how she found the note in her box. Oh, and Laura Salvo, and—"

"Okay, okay," George agreed, laughing at Nancy's eagerness. "But you'd better lie down while you make your calls. I'll make some soup and get your clothes clean. You're a mess."

"George," Nancy said, as they headed north toward Old Town, "who from the show could have set that fire? Who was missing from the studio today?"

"Practically everyone," George told her with a frown. "Right after you and Lieutenant Dunne left, the Sterns assembled everyone in the studio. They announced that taping was suspended until further notice because the insurance company had insisted on it. There'll be no more shows until—"

"Until we catch the people behind this," Nancy finished for her. "And if we don't do it fast, the show will be history.

"So who do you think is behind all this, George?" Nancy continued.

"Don't ask me," George said with a crooked grin. "You're the detective."

"Samantha Savage and Vic Molina were in that garage together," Nancy said. "Why? We don't know. Then there's that note I found the night of the benefit—the one from Samantha's friend Mort, whoever he is. Vic had that date with her, though. That's what bothers me."

"Huh?" George said. "I don't get it."

"If they're working together to sabotage 'Marcy!' why advertise the fact by having a very public date together? Secret meetings in a parking garage, yes, but not a date at a big party. Besides, neither of them works at Stern Productions."

They parked on Susan's street and let themselves into her apartment. Susan wasn't home, but there was a message from her on the machine. "Hi," her voice announced, "I'm at Marcy's because she's really upset. I'll call later. 'Bye."

"Poor Marcy," George said.

Nancy shook her head sadly. "I'm going to get cleaned up," she said, heading for the shower. But as she stood under the running water, a sudden spell of dizziness overtook her. "Whoa," she said out loud. "I'd better go lie down."

She threw on her robe, went to the living room, and lay down on the futon. A few minutes later George came in and set down a bowl of hot soup next to her.

"You really look terrible," George said. "Are you sure you're okay, Nan?"

"I'm fine, I'm fine," Nancy insisted. Then, seeing that George wasn't going to leave her alone, Nancy added, "Could you go get me some magazines to read, George? I think I'll take your advice and stay in bed this evening."

"Good idea," George agreed.

After George left, Nancy quickly got to work. She found Laura's number and dialed it, but she wasn't home. Nancy left a message to call her at Susan's. The Sterns' number was unlisted. Nancy jotted down a note to see them first thing in the morning. Then, and only then, did she dial Lieutenant Dunne's number.

The lieutenant had already been briefed on the fire by the crew on the scene. "Look here, Nancy," he said in a worried voice. "This is dangerous. From now on, I want to know your whereabouts every second of the day. I've already got a guard on Marcy Robbins, maybe I ought to put one on you, too."

"I can take care of myself, Lieutenant Dunne," Nancy insisted. "I'll be much more careful from now on, I promise. By the way, did you get a report on the fingerprints? The ones on the marker?"

"Oh, that," the lieutenant said. "Yes, I did. We got two sets of prints. One was the cleaning lady's. The other didn't match up with any in our criminal files."

"Well, of course not," Nancy said, trying to mask her impatience. "We're not dealing with career criminals here, Lieutenant. Can't we get prints on everyone who works at Stern Productions?"

"Nancy," the lieutenant said, stopping her. "Even if we could, the marker would only be circumstantial evidence. Who's to say it's the marker that was used to write the note? By the way, the pay phone had no prints on it—neither did the scarf. Now that they won't be taping the show for the time being, we shouldn't have any new mischief to contend with."

"Let's hope not," Nancy said. "But if the show does shut down permanently, it means that the criminals will have succeeded. We can't let that happen!"

"Don't get carried away, Nancy," Lieutenant Dunne said. "It's my job to save lives and keep the public order, not to see that a TV show stays on the air."

Nancy said goodbye and hung up just as George reentered with the magazines. "I'm going down to the basement to wash our clothes," George said, gathering up Nancy's smoky outfit and adding some of her own things.

Nancy picked up the latest issue of

Primetime, the entertainment news weekly. The issue was dated for the coming Monday, Nancy noticed.

On the cover was a picture of Gene Martinez and Carol Bell, the stars of "Southern Star" and "Miller's Dream." Apparently, the two had a real-life romance that was leading them to the altar.

Nancy read the article, which showed a picture of the happy couple, along with a relaxed-looking Vic Molina. "We picked Vic Molina as our best man because he's been such a good friend," Carol was quoted as saying in the article. "Vic is a warm, caring person," Gene agreed. "He's a great guy and a terrific producer."

Vic Molina obviously inspired loyalty in people, Nancy thought. Even Marcy had nice things to say about him.

Next, the name *Marcy Robbins,* in boldface type, caught Nancy's eye.

Marcy's was one of the names mentioned in "Let's Dish," a gossip column written by Lydia Luster.

Let's dish about Marcy Robbins. I don't care how young she is, she sure has managed to make lots of enemies. Rumor has it her producers are getting cold feet about signing her on for more shows, despite her ratings. According to a very naughty little songbird I know, contracts will be offered to the show's NEW HOST the day this magazine hits the stands!

Nancy's eyes widened. Someone was going to replace Marcy! Was it too late for Nancy to solve the case? Had time run out?

Chapter

Eleven

NANCY BLINKED HARD and gritted her teeth. A new host for "Marcy!"? It couldn't be happening. She couldn't let it happen! She reread the article.

"'According to a very naughty little songbird'—that has to be Samantha Savage," Nancy said out loud. "Now, how would she know about Marcy being replaced before anyone else does?"

Nancy thought hard. If it was true, it meant that the Sterns must have gone looking for a new host as soon as there was trouble. Not very loyal of them, Nancy couldn't help thinking.

One thing, though—Samantha Savage seemed to be involved. She could be the key to the whole mystery if Nancy could get her to tell what she knew.

Nancy's gaze fell to the bottom of Lydia Luster's column, where two more names in boldface caught her eye.

Samantha Savage and Vic Molina are scheduled to have their big date as this magazine hits the stands. After sailing on Lake Michigan and eating at fabulous El Chizote, it'll be a hot night of dancing at Parallelogram. Between dances, Samantha will autograph free posters of herself for buyers of her new CD. So even on a hot date Samantha Savage is all business. Look for exclusive pix next week.

Nancy bounded out of bed, flushed with excitement. All the new information she'd taken in buzzed through her head. First of all, the magazine was dated for the next Monday, but today was Wednesday. According to the article, Vic and Samantha were on their big date on that very day, at that very moment! If they had been sailing that afternoon, neither of them could have set the fire. They would have been surrounded by reporters and photographers everywhere they went.

Of course, that didn't mean they weren't behind the threats. They could have been working with someone at Stern Productions, and *that* person could have set the fire.

All along, Vic and Samantha had been at the center of Nancy's suspicions. It was time to put those suspicions to the test.

A plan began forming in Nancy's mind as she put on clean clothes and fresh makeup. By the time George got back with the laundry, Nancy was ready for action.

"George, we're going out," she announced, walking up to her friend and taking the laundry from her hands. "I'll put this with our stuff while you read the *Primetime* on the bed—the 'Let's Dish' column, second paragraph."

"Huh?" George said, but picked up the magazine and read it, wide-eyed. "A new host?" she cried. "How can that be? It's so soon, and how did 'a naughty songbird' find out about it?"

"That's what I'd like to know!" Nancy said. She checked her watch. It was seven-thirty. "Come on, George. We're going to Parallelogram."

"You're sure you're up to dancing?" George asked, concerned.

"I'm not going to be dancing, George—*you* are." Nancy gave her friend a wink. "Get changed, okay? Put on your best dress."

George did as she was told. "Nancy, I don't like that gleam in your eye one bit. What are you cooking up?"

Nancy giggled. "You're going to make a perfect spectacle of yourself, George. By this time tomorrow, your face will be on the cover of every tabloid in Chicago!"

The girls got the address of Parallelogram from the telephone book, and by the time they'd found the place and parked, it was past eight o'clock. The club, on a wide boulevard shaded by trees, was open for business. Still, it was early, and even though Samantha Savage was scheduled to be there, the line in front wasn't all that long. Nancy and George found themselves inside in just ten minutes.

"Business must be slow, George," Nancy said, flashing her friend a quick smile. "But you'll fix that. Just remember the plan. When you see Vic and Samantha dancing together, you cut in and steal Vic away. Flirt with him. The idea is to stir up trouble, so Samantha will get mad enough to say things she didn't mean to say."

George shook her head and made a face. "I wish Bess were here," she said with a sigh. "She's the one for this job, not me."

"Oh, come on," Nancy chided her. "I know you've got it in you."

It was impossible to talk while the music was playing, so when Nancy spotted Samantha at a table, signing photos of herself, Nancy motioned for George to follow her. In back of the table was a large pillar, and Nancy led George to it so they could listen without being seen.

Vic Molina was standing next to Samantha. To Nancy, he seemed bored, if not downright annoyed.

On Samantha's other side was an extremely fat bald man with a mustache, wearing a brown business suit. He seemed to be in charge, coaching Samantha with little whispers in her ear every now and then.

Between songs, Samantha pulled the fat man aside. "Mort," she said furiously. "This is humiliating. There's nobody here! You were supposed to make sure hundreds of people showed up."

Mort? So this was the writer of the note Nancy had found at the celebrity auction!

"I'm your manager, honey, not a magician," the man said. "I gave the information to the papers, but it was too late. You should have told me last week you wanted to sign photos on this date."

"I didn't *think* of it till yesterday!" Samantha snapped. "And why did you volunteer me for this stupid charity date with Vic, anyway?"

"Hey, I thought you wanted to go out with him. The guy's the hottest producer on TV, and you want your own series eventually, don't you? Besides, he's a hunk, and he's Marcy Robbins's old boyfriend. What could be better, huh? Why don't you dance with the guy once? He's bored to tears." Mort puffed up his cheeks in frustration.

"He's still in love with Marcy, that's why," Samantha said hotly. "All through dinner he moaned and groaned about how she dropped him."

"But he's suing her," Mort said. "I don't get it."

"It's crazy, I know," Samantha agreed. She kept on talking, but just then the music picked up again. Mort covered his ears, and he and Samantha went back to the table. Samantha signed two more autographs for the only fans waiting, then went over to Vic and dragged him onto the dance floor, making sure that the photographers caught them. Nancy saw Vic shake his head, objecting, but Samantha was insistent, and soon they were dancing up a storm.

After a minute or two the music seemed to work its magic on Vic, and he looked like he was enjoying himself. Samantha was flirting with him outrageously, and Mort was smiling like a contented cat from the sidelines, his hands still over his ears.

"Now!" Nancy cued George, and gave her a little shove. Rolling her eyes and shaking her head, George threaded her way through the dancing couples on the floor till she got to Vic and Samantha. First, she caught the producer's eye. Then, in one swift and graceful motion, she touched Vic's elbow and turned him toward her, maneuvering herself between Vic and Samantha. Vic didn't resist. In fact, he smiled and started dancing with George as camera strobes flashed all over the room.

Samantha had been stopped dead. As she stood there, Nancy could almost see the smoke pouring from her ears. "How dare you, Vic Molina?" Samantha growled. "You're trying to make me a laughingstock!"

Everyone backed away from them as the cameras kept ticking. Vic froze, while George took off in the direction of the rest rooms. Nancy edged forward to hear and see better. George had done her job perfectly.

"Samantha, control yourself, okay?" Vic told her, trying to keep his voice down. "The girl just grabbed my hand. What was I supposed to do?"

"Don't give me that!" Samantha shrieked. "You didn't say one word the whole dinner that wasn't 'Marcy Robbins, Marcy Robbins.'"

"I told you, I feel sorry for her," Vic tried to explain.

Mort had come up behind his client and was trying to restrain her. "Sammy, dear, there are reporters here. Remember your image, sweetheart."

This seemed to get Samantha's attention. She turned toward the cameras that were aimed at her, but she still spat out her words. "You can put this in all your papers—Vic Molina is going to be the new coproducer of 'Marcy!'—he told me so—only it won't be called 'Marcy!' anymore—"

"Sam, be quiet!" Mort ordered, his face going livid as Vic's face went dead white. "Nobody's supposed to know. You'll ruin everything."

"Here's your scoop, friends," she went on, breaking free of Mort's grip and advancing on the cluster of reporters and photographers. "The new show is going to be called 'Bore Me to Tears' because Vic and his coproducers, the Sterns, are going to sign the most boring person in the universe to be the new host!"

"Sammy, you said you didn't want to host a TV talk show!" Mort protested.

"I didn't," Samantha said. Then she turned to Vic, who was still standing there, shaking with rage, his hands balled into fists. "But honestly, Vic—you could have at least offered me the job!" With that, she stormed off in Nancy's direction, muttering to herself.

"Who? Who is it, Samantha?" the reporters were yelling. Only Nancy, who was right next to Samantha as she stalked away, heard what she said.

"Of all people—talk about boring—even Marcy Robbins is better than Karen Kristoff—"

Karen Kristoff! Nancy gasped when she heard the name. The gasp drew Vic Molina's attention, and his eyes lit on Nancy.

"Hey," he said, suddenly coming alert. "I know you—you're the one from the parking lot!" Vic snarled, backing her up against the pillar and grabbing her arm. "Just exactly who are you?"

Chapter
Twelve

AT THAT MOMENT a blur in a green dress flew at Vic Molina, barreling into him and knocking him aside. It was George. "Run for it, Nancy!" she yelled as she headed for the exit.

Nancy raced after her, and the two girls were down the street and in the car before anyone ran out of the club after them. George hit the gas, and that was the end of any pursuit.

"Well, you really stirred up a storm, George," Nancy told her friend. "Samantha told the whole world that Vic Molina is going to coproduce a new talk show with the Sterns."

"So I guess that makes him look pretty guilty, huh?" George said.

"Maybe," Nancy said. "I found out something else, too. Something no one else overheard Samantha say—the new host of the show is going to be Karen Kristoff."

"Karen?" George asked. "Why her? She doesn't have any experience in television, does she?"

"I don't think so," Nancy said. "But neither did Marcy. At any rate, this makes Karen Kristoff a suspect."

"I suppose so," George had to agree.

"Besides which, Karen fired Laura Salvo. Why?" Nancy asked pointedly. "Only someone who knew we had talked to Laura could have written that note luring me to the fire! I think we're going to have a little chat with Karen Kristoff first thing in the morning."

"And just how are we going to do that?" George wanted to know.

"We've got a scoop, here, George," Nancy explained. "Now all we have to do is become instant reporters."

"But, Nan, she's already met us," George reminded her.

"Only as friends of Susan Ling's—that's how we were introduced at the celebrity auction. Who says we're not visiting reporters from, oh, say, *River Heights Scene?*"

"What's that?" George asked.

"It's a magazine I just invented," Nancy quipped.

* * *

When they got back to Susan's, their friend was already there. "What in the world happened?" she asked impatiently as they came in. "There are all kinds of messages for you on the machine. Did George give you the note Laura left in my box?"

"Yes—only it wasn't from Laura," Nancy said.

Susan's eyes grew wide.

"Sit down, Susan," Nancy said, leading her to the sofa. "It's a long story."

After telling it, Nancy went to the answering machine and listened to the messages. There was one from Brenda Fox. "Hi, Nancy," it said. "I know you're investigating everything that's been happening to Marcy, and I just wanted to tell you something weird. It may be nothing, but this afternoon I got a phone call telling me to pick up some papers at the Sterns' accounting firm. When I got there, the accountants didn't know anything about it. It's almost as if someone wanted me out of the studio. Do you think something funny is going on?"

"I sure do," Nancy replied as the message clicked off. Either Brenda was lying to account for her absence from the studio, Nancy reflected, or else somebody was trying to throw suspicion on her.

There was also a brief message from Laura

Salvo. Nancy jotted down the number and dialed it.

"Hello?" Laura's voice said over the wire.

"Laura? This is Nancy Drew."

"Oh, Susan Ling's friend, right," Laura said. "I never did find those files. I don't know if you heard, but—"

"You were fired. I know," Nancy told her. "I'm really sorry."

"Oh, that's okay." Laura was silent for a moment. "I guess I'd been there long enough, anyway. But it was strange—"

"What do you mean?" Nancy asked quickly.

"Well, Ms. Kristoff got incredibly upset when she found out that I was looking for those files. She called me into her office and got really mad at me." Now Laura's voice started to tremble. "She said my work wasn't up to her standards, but I don't buy that."

"I don't either," Nancy said firmly. "Something else is going on. You just got drawn into it."

Nancy heard Laura sigh.

"You didn't leave a message for me to meet you today, did you?" Nancy asked.

"A message?" Laura said. "No, I'm afraid not."

"Thanks," Nancy told her, and hung up. "Do you have a tape recorder, Sue? A little one?"

"Sure," Susan said.

"Can I borrow it and a camera, if you have one."

"Only an instant camera," Susan replied. "Will that be good enough?"

"It'll have to do," Nancy said. "Thanks. We'll take good care of them, I promise."

"Whose picture are you going to take?" Susan asked.

"Karen Kristoff's," Nancy told her. "If she's replacing Marcy, she has a motive. If she's got a motive, she's a suspect."

First thing the next morning Susan dropped Nancy and George off in front of the offices of *Teen Talk.* The girls checked out their reflections in the polished black granite before going upstairs.

"May I help you?" a henna-haired receptionist asked Nancy and George when they stepped up to the little window.

"Yes, we're from *River Heights Scene,*" Nancy fibbed. "We're here to interview Karen Kristoff."

The receptionist buzzed them in and called the editor's office.

Soon Karen appeared. The bright red of her blouse perfectly matched her scarlet lips and fingertips. Eyeing Nancy and George carefully through a too friendly smile, she said, "Don't I know you girls?"

"We sat at the same table at the benefit the

other night," Nancy said. "We're friends of Susan Ling's. We're also with *River Heights Scene*—it's a brand-new magazine. Our first issue is coming up soon, and when we heard you were going to replace Marcy Robbins, we just had to have an interview!"

"Where did you hear that?" Karen asked, her eyes narrowed.

"Oh, everybody's talking about it!" Nancy gushed.

"Oh, yes," George agreed. "And with Vic Molina producing it, it'll be fantastic! We're going to try to interview him later."

Karen recovered from her initial surprise quickly. "Well, I'm afraid I haven't got time for an interview this morning," she said sweetly. "Besides, nothing's finalized yet, and until a deal is on paper, you know . . ."

"Oh, of course. We understand," Nancy assured her. "We won't spoil anything for you, we promise. Right, George?"

"Right, Nancy," George said. "Right, Ms. Kristoff."

Karen gave them a funny look, and Nancy wondered if Karen didn't guess they were pretending. Then a big smile came over her face again, as if the other look had never been there.

"Oh, all right. Come on into my office. But just a few quick questions and that's it. I've got to be out of here by eleven if I want to make a meeting." Karen led them to a crowded corner office with a view of Lake Shore Drive.

"Pardon the mess," Karen said with a small laugh as she took a seat behind her paper-strewn desk. "Now, first you tell me where you heard I was replacing Marcy Robbins." She gave them another big smile.

"Good reporters never divulge their sources, Ms. Kristoff," Nancy interrupted. "And any information you give us will be held confidential until you say it's okay to print it."

Karen gave Nancy a nod. "You're quite the reporter, aren't you?"

"Now, about the big offer?" Nancy prompted her.

"As I said, I can't confirm any offer because so far I haven't been given any firm deal."

"We heard Marcy was extremely upset," George said, beginning the interview as she brought out her tape recorder. "May I turn this on?"

Karen hesitated before nodding. "I do feel awful about Marcy," Karen said, shaking her head. "After the bomb threat, she was just too great a security risk. At least, that's what everyone said. In any case, it was bound to happen sooner or later. Marcy wasn't cut out for TV. She was much more effective as a print journalist, if you ask me."

"You went to the same high school as Marcy, didn't you?" Nancy asked, suppressing the urge to argue with Karen.

"Well, yes," Karen said. "You've done your research. I'm impressed."

"It must be exciting to go from editor to TV journalist," George said enthusiastically. "Have you ever been on TV before?"

"Actually, I've been a guest on a number of talk shows, and I briefly had a radio talk show. Still, this will be a wonderful opportunity for growth."

"What will you call the show?" George asked.

"Now, that would be getting way ahead of myself," Karen said. Checking her watch, she added, "I really am pressed this morning, girls. Why don't you call me tomorrow. I should know more by then." Karen got up and indicated the door, leaving no doubt that the interview was over.

As she rose to go, Nancy took in the wall covered with enlarged color photos across the room. Most were of Karen with various celebrities. Something in one of the photos caught Nancy's eye. She stood up quickly. "Ms. Kristoff, can we get a picture to go with the interview?"

"Well, I suppose that wouldn't hurt," Karen said. When she spotted George's instant camera, she frowned. "Is that all you brought? It won't take a magazine-quality picture, you know."

"Yes, w-well," George stammered, "we're operating on a very low budget."

Karen gave her a condescending smile. "I understand, dear," she said. "It's all right."

"George, take her over here, by this wall, okay?" Nancy said, indicating the wall of photos.

Karen posed for a series of shots while Nancy and George chatted about the new show.

Nancy could barely suppress a triumphant smile as the editor said goodbye. When she and George were outside the building, Nancy said, "Let's take a look at that photo you just snapped. The colors are just coming in now— there. Look at the wall behind Karen. The big color enlargement of her with the stars of 'Miller's Dream.'"

"I'm looking," George said, squinting in the bright morning sunlight. "But I guess I'm not seeing what you are."

"What's Karen wearing around her neck?" Nancy prompted her friend.

"A paisley scarf," George replied. "So wh— ohhhh! Is that the one you found?"

"That's the one," Nancy said. "See the red

and black, with the gold thread pattern around the edges?"

"Uh-huh," George said. "But, Nan, that means—"

"That's right," Nancy told her. "We've found our mystery caller. And her name is Karen Kristoff!"

Chapter

Thirteen

"Wow!" George gasped. "Fantastic, Nan. We've broken open the case!" Then she paused for a second. "So what do we do now?"

"First things first, George," Nancy said. "We have to contact Lieutenant Dunne and tell him what we've found."

Pointing to a pay phone at the corner, Nancy led George to it and called the lieutenant at police headquarters. To Nancy's surprise Dunne didn't seem very impressed.

"So you saw it in a photograph," he said. "What does that prove? It's circumstantial at best—like that purple marker."

"Magenta," Nancy corrected him, barely containing her annoyance. "Have you checked the Stern employees' fingerprints yet?"

"Nancy," the lieutenant answered impatiently, "we're doing all we can over here. Without more evidence, I can't fingerprint two dozen people. I'd get my head handed to me on a platter."

"Can't you question Karen Kristoff, at least?" Nancy prodded him. "Maybe she'd confess under pressure or reveal the name of her partner at Stern Productions, the one who rigged the TelePrompTer and tore up Marcy's picture."

"Whoa there, you're going too fast, Nancy," the lieutenant cautioned her. "Look, you're talking about the media here. The *national* media. If I step on anybody's toes, and they turn out to be innocent, I could be kissing my whole career goodbye."

"Meanwhile, Marcy's career is gone," Nancy said hotly. "I suppose that's okay with you."

"Now, now," Dunne returned, "don't get like that. I'll do another round of questioning in the next day or so, and I'll include Kristoff with the others, all right? It'll all get straightened out sooner or later."

"And what about Marcy?" Nancy insisted.

"I've still got a guard on her," Dunne reassured her. "And if Marcy's any good, she'll come back from this. She's young. There'll be plenty of other chances."

Nancy hung up, steaming. "Ooooh, he makes me so mad!" she burst out. "George, we're going to have to tackle Karen Kristoff ourselves."

"What do you mean, Nan?" George asked, taken aback.

"Lieutenant Dunne is obviously more concerned with his own reputation than with solving this case. I think he's hoping that now that the show's canceled, the problem will just go away."

"Didn't he think the scarf was proof?" George asked.

"The guy seems to want a confession, signed, sealed, and delivered," Nancy said. "So we're going to give it to him."

"Huh?"

"I've got a plan," Nancy said, slinging an arm around her friend's shoulders and leading her back to the Media Center. "Karen said she's going to a meeting at eleven. We're going to send her on a little detour."

"But we're going the wrong way, Nan," George protested. "Karen's office is back there."

"We've got almost an hour," Nancy explained, "and I want to stop off at the Stern offices first. Now, here's what we're going to do. . . ."

The mood at the Stern offices was glum. From the security guard, who recognized them, to Ginger and Dee and Brenda—everyone was wearing a long face.

Susan was at her desk, gathering up her personal stuff. The Sterns were nowhere in sight, and neither was Marcy. "She just couldn't bear to come in today," Susan explained when Nancy asked. "She called me this morning after you left. She said to thank you both for trying to help."

"That's awful!" George exclaimed. "Poor Marcy."

"Susan," Nancy said, handing her the snapshot. "Could you do me a favor and deliver this to Lieutenant Dunne—in person?"

Susan glanced at the photo and shrugged. "Sure, Nancy. I'll be done here in a few minutes, and I've got the whole day free after that."

"We all do," said Jack Cole, who was coming down the corridor toward them. "And all day tomorrow and the day after that." Jack was obviously depressed, too. "Poor Marcy," he said, shaking his head. "I wonder how she is. Have any of you spoken to her?"

"I have," Susan said, and she told him what Marcy had said about not coming in to clean out her stuff.

Jack seemed troubled. "Gee," he said, "I wonder why she didn't call me?" Nancy could see the hurt in his eyes. "Hmm," he went on thoughtfully. "I guess I should go visit her to cheer her up."

"I don't know if she's ready for that," Susan said cautiously.

Jack stared at her. "You don't know her like I do," he said before turning and walking away, his walkie-talkie bouncing in its holster. Nancy noticed the muscles on his arms. Athletic, she said to herself.

"Weird guy," Susan remarked, taking the photo from Nancy and putting it in an envelope before placing it in her shoulder bag. "He sure cares about Marcy, though."

There was caring and then there was caring, Nancy thought to herself, but she didn't say anything. She was getting an uneasy feeling about Jack Cole and wondered what his real feelings were toward Marcy. He didn't seem to have any reason to harm her, but . . .

Nancy took comfort in the knowledge that Marcy had a police officer guarding her at all times. "I guess we're done here," she told Susan. "George and I have to go someplace, Susan. I don't know when we'll be done, but where can we reach you?"

"At home, I guess," Susan said. "Or at Marcy's. If she's ready to talk, I want to be there for her. She's not just my boss, she's my friend, too. And I can't stand to see this happen to her." Susan angrily wiped a stray tear from her cheek.

"Neither can we," Nancy told her. "And we're not going to let it happen."

"But it already has, Nancy!" Susan protested. "They're replacing her with Karen Kristoff, aren't they?"

"Not if George and I can help it," Nancy replied.

Nancy and George stood in the corner of the lobby of the *Teen Talk* building, reading newspapers that they held up high to hide their faces. When Karen Kristoff emerged from the elevator and headed for the revolving doors, the two girls were right behind her.

Karen walked about three blocks, then turned left. "Look!" George whispered to Nancy when the girls turned the corner after her. "It's Pepe's Garage! She's going in, Nan!"

Sure enough, Karen Kristoff was already heading down the ramp. Nancy started running with George following. Pepe was nowhere in sight as the girls went inside. On the first level down, they saw Karen opening her car door.

"Now, George!" Nancy whispered, breaking into a run. Karen Kristoff was just pulling the door to her gold car closed. "Karen, wait!" Nancy yelled, flying over and holding the door open. "We need to talk to you, *right now!*"

Karen flinched, her face dead white. "Why

are you following me around?" she asked. "I met with you, didn't I? I told you, I have to get to a meeting!" She yanked violently on the door, trying to close it, but Nancy held firm.

"We know about the meeting," Nancy told her. "And we also know what you've done to Marcy." Nancy stared at her until the editor's lip began to tremble.

"You're not reporters, are you?" she said, her voice breaking. "I knew something was off about you two."

"That's right, Karen," Nancy said coolly. "I'm a detective working for Marcy Robbins."

Karen's hand moved and turned on the ignition. As she did, George ran in front of the car. Nancy saw Karen hesitate and knew she wouldn't run George down. George knew it, too.

"We've already given the police concrete evidence against you," Nancy warned Karen. "They've got the scarf you lost when you made that threatening phone call, and it's been identified as yours. It won't be long before they come for you." Karen's face was crumbling now. She leaned back in the driver's seat, and turned the ignition off. "Look, Karen, why don't we climb in there with you. We can talk more privately. Maybe we can even help."

Karen nodded and scooted over to the passenger side. Nancy got behind the wheel, and

George sat in back. "There," Nancy said when they had closed the doors, and she heard the click of the tape recorder being turned on by George. "That's better. Now, Karen, if you'll tell us how it happened, and who's working with you, I promise we'll put in a good word with the police on your behalf."

"I—I don't—know if—" Karen could barely get the words out.

"It'll be all right," Nancy said soothingly. "After all, you did call to warn Marcy about your accomplice. Didn't you?"

Karen nodded slowly. "Yes," she said, barely whispering. "I made all the phone threats. But that's all I did. Honestly!" Her voice was rising now, as she pleaded with them for understanding. "I never meant it to get out of hand, I swear! I just wanted her to quit the show, so they'd give it to me."

"What made you think they'd give Marcy's job to you?" Nancy wanted to know.

"Because they almost offered it to me the first time, that's why!" Karen cried. "It should have been mine to begin with, not hers! I'm older than she is—I gave her her first big break, for goodness sake. And then, she takes the job I've wanted all my life!"

She turned to Nancy, pleading again. "We grew up together, she and Jack and I. We all knew one another and would always talk about what big successes we'd be." She frowned. "I hate her," she said softly. "She's ruined my life."

"You've ruined it yourself," George put in. "If you hadn't made those threats—"

"I couldn't help it!" Karen shouted. "I was just—so—*angry.*" She shuddered and sighed. "But I never meant to hurt anybody. The phony bomb? That wasn't me—in fact, he wanted to use a real one. He's crazy. Breaking into people's apartments and setting buildings on fire—"

"Who? Who's crazy?" Nancy asked impatiently. "Unless you tell us, Karen, you'll be helping a criminal do more harm."

Karen hesitated. "He'll kill me if I say," she whimpered.

"Just tell me if I guess right," Nancy said soothingly. "It had to be someone with access to Marcy and the studio," she reasoned. "Someone Marcy thought of as a friend, who could change the message on the TelePrompTer and plant a phony bomb. Someone athletic enough to climb to Susan Ling's terrace and crazy enough to set that fire. Someone you've known for years. It's Jack Cole, isn't it, Karen?"

Slowly Karen nodded. "Yes," she whispered. "He's always loved Marcy. From the beginning. More than loved her, he's obsessed by her. Oh, he hid it well, but when she rejected him—"

"Rejected him?" Nancy stopped her. "What do you mean?"

"They went out for a short time, in senior year," Karen explained. "Marcy told him she just wanted to be friends. So he stayed friends with her. And he never told her how she'd broken his heart.

"That's how Jack is—hidden. But he cried on my shoulder plenty of times. And when Marcy broke *my* heart, just like she broke his—"

Karen stopped for a second. Nancy nodded, encouraging her to go on. Then Karen said, "I knew people would start snooping around. That's why I pulled those files about us all growing up together in Cicero. I was afraid someone would connect me with Jack Cole. When Laura Salvo told me she was looking for the files, I had to get rid of her. I thought that would be the end of it. It would have been, too, except then Jack heard the police lieutenant say you were a detective.

"From that moment on, Jack flipped out totally. I told him that you'd contacted Laura, and that got him even crazier. He told me he wanted you dead. He got paranoid that you'd find out what we were up to.

"See, all I wanted was for Marcy to be taken off the show so I'd get her job. But Jack felt that if Marcy's career were totally lost, she'd go to him, and he could get her to love him the way he loves her. He's crazy, I'm telling you. That's why I made that warning call. I knew he was going to try to kill somebody. I—"

"I understand," Nancy told her. "You've done yourself a lot of good by being honest. Now we're going to Marcy's. If I'm right, we've got no time to lose. Do you know where she lives?"

"Of course I do," Karen said flatly. All the life seemed to have gone out of her. Nancy turned the key in the ignition and the engine roared. "Marcy and I used to be best friends."

Following Karen's directions, Nancy drove them to the Near North Side, and Marcy's town house, a graceful old building on a tree-lined street.

"I want to make sure she's okay," Nancy explained, unbuckling her seat belt. "You stay in the car with George while I go check. Is that okay with you, George?" Nancy asked.

"Sure," George replied. "I'll just move up front."

Nancy left them in the car and advanced on the front door. Fear rose in her heart. Was the police guard who had been assigned to Marcy inside? Jack Cole had said he was coming to see Marcy. Was he still here?

The door opened at Nancy's touch—a bad sign. Nancy walked into the living room and gasped. A woman was lying on the floor, bound and gagged.

It was Susan Ling!

Chapter

Fourteen

Even as Nancy cried out in surprise, she was on her knees untying the ropes. A huge sob burst from Susan as Nancy pulled the gag out of her mouth.

"Oh, Na-ancy," she said, her voice catching, "Jack Cole—he ti-ied me up and took Marcy with him!" She began sobbing again.

"Calm down, Susan," Nancy said, stroking the young woman's hair and holding her. "It's going to be all right. We're going to save Marcy. But you have to calm down. We don't have much time."

Susan got the message. With great effort, she managed to catch her breath.

"Susan, Karen Kristoff made the phone threats. She and Jack were working together. George is outside in the car with her."

"Oh!" Susan put her hand over her mouth in alarm. "The picture—Jack took it. The photo you gave me—"

"Don't worry, Susan," Nancy reassured her. "We've already got a taped confession. Now, about Jack. Tell me everything."

Before Susan could begin, though, Nancy heard a siren approaching, then a car screech to a halt in front of Marcy's house. In a matter of seconds, Lieutenant Dunne burst through the front door. He ran over to Nancy. "Everything all right?" he asked, looking from Nancy to Susan. "Somebody called the officer I had assigned here and told him I wanted him to report to headquarters."

"Marcy's been kidnapped by Jack Cole," Nancy said quickly. "He's the one who set the fire and made the bomb threat, too. Karen Kristoff made the phone threats, as I told you. She's in the car out front, with George, and we've got a taped confession from her."

"What?" The lieutenant looked every bit as stunned as he must have felt. "I—well, I—good work, Nancy. Thank you."

"You're welcome, Lieutenant," Nancy told him. "We need to work together now. We've got to save Marcy."

Susan began by telling them what had happened. "When I showed up, Jack was here with Marcy. I don't know what was going on, but when he saw me, he pulled a gun."

"He's armed and dangerous," Dunne told one of the officers who had come up behind him and heard the last part of the conversation. "Check to see if Ms. Robbins's car is here. Then get the license number and make of Jack Cole's car right away."

"It's a dark gray hatchback, Lieutenant," Susan said. "With a dent in the front right fender."

"You heard her," Dunne said to his officers. "Put out an all-points bulletin for Marcy Robbins, traveling with a Caucasian male, thin build, brown hair, light eyes. I want them found—fast! Oh, and see that gold coupe over there? Ms. Karen Kristoff is inside. Take her down to headquarters and book her."

The officers took off as Dunne turned to the girls. "You were saying?" he asked Susan, pulling out a pad and pencil to make notes.

"He made Marcy get rope and tape for him, and then he tied me up. He said he and Marcy were in love with each other and were going to go away together. She looked terrified."

Nancy put a comforting hand on Susan's shoulder. "Did he say anything else, Susan?" she asked. "Anything that could help us figure out where he took her?"

Susan concentrated hard, biting her lip. Then she shrugged helplessly. "I don't know. I don't remember his exact words at all."

"Maybe they'll come back to you later,"

Dunne suggested. "I'll want to get more details later, Miss Ling. Right now, I have to get to work."

Nancy and Susan said goodbye to the lieutenant and walked out onto the sidewalk, where George approached them. "The police told me what happened. I can't believe it! What are we going to do?"

"You have your car here, right, Susan?" Nancy asked.

"I sure do," Susan replied.

"Let's all get in it and talk," Nancy said.

Susan led them to her car. "They wouldn't still be anywhere near here," Susan said once they settled themselves inside. "He would have taken her far away."

"Not necessarily," Nancy said, thinking hard. "But I bet you're right about one thing. They're nowhere near here. Let's think, guys. Jack is in love with Marcy, he's obsessed with her. He thinks if he can get her to leave her show, she'll finally come back to him."

"Okay, so far so good," George agreed. "They stop taping the show, and a new host is hired. Marcy's career is in ruins. Now what?"

"Jack hears that Marcy's heartbroken. Now's his chance," Nancy said, leaning forward eagerly. "He can be the one to console her! So he goes to her and tells her how he feels—how he's felt all along . . ."

"But she doesn't feel the same about him," George added.

Susan chimed in. "So he goes crazy and tells her he's going to take her away to their own dark little world. That's when I walked in."

Nancy gasped, and grabbed Susan's elbow hard. "Susan!" she said, her heart racing. "What you just said—were those Jack's words? *Their own dark little world.*"

"I think so," Susan murmured.

Nancy's eyes lit up. "I think I know where Jack's taken Marcy!"

"Where?" George asked excitedly.

"To the underground tunnels they used to hang out in when they were growing up," Nancy said. "He told me about them backstage at the celebrity auction. He said they were in Cicero."

"Cicero, here we come," Susan said, revving the engine and pulling the car into the street.

"Of course," George remarked. "That's exactly where he would take her. To a place they shared. It's romantic but creepy at the same time."

"With a heavy emphasis on the creepy," Susan added as she took the ramp for the expressway.

When they reached Cicero, Nancy saw that it was a neighborhood of modest clapboard houses bunched closely together. There didn't seem to be anything extraordinary about it, as far as Nancy could tell.

Then she saw something she recognized. "The racetrack!" she shouted. "Jack told me a tunnel entrance was there!"

Quickly Susan pointed the car toward the track. Five blocks later they passed a narrow alleyway, and Susan jammed on the brakes. "Look!" she cried, pointing. "That's Jack's car! See the dent?"

They pulled over and ran to the car, which was locked and empty. "Susan, go call the police. Tell Lieutenant Dunne to hurry, okay?"

"Right, Nan," Susan said.

"George, doesn't that building on the other side of the fence look like a stable?" Nancy said, pointing toward the end of the alley where a chain-link fence ran beside what appeared to be the back end of the racetrack. "Jack told me that the tunnel was near a stable," she explained, her voice pitched high with excitement.

"We'll need a flashlight," she said then. "Have you got one in the car, Susan?"

"Aren't you lucky? We gofers carry everything," Susan said with a grin, popping open the trunk and giving Nancy a sturdy, powerful flashlight. "Good luck, you two," she said as she got in the driver's seat and drove off to find a phone.

"Come on, George," Nancy said, heading for the fence, the flashlight in her hand.

"What do the tunnel entrances look like, Nan?" George asked.

"I don't know," Nancy said, as she squirmed through a gap in the fence. Once inside, she led her friend toward the stable. There were a lot of people at the track, but all their attention was on the race in progress. In the distance, Nancy heard the announcer's voice and the cheers as the horses raced for the finish.

Luckily, there was no one right around them. They peeked in an open doorway. The building was a stable—but an old, unused one. "At least we won't be seen," Nancy said.

Hay covered the ground around the stable and the dry particles drifted up with the dry dirt. "Ick, Nan, this is disgusting," George said, brushing at her already dusty clothes.

"George, I have a feeling the tunnels are going to be worse, but they'll be wet probably," Nancy warned her friend. "Hey, what's that?"

When they rounded the far corner of the stable, Nancy saw a small, fenced-in area about eight feet around. Inside the fence was an iron hatchway. Lifting the lid, they saw a ladder leading down. "Looks like a tunnel entrance to me," George said. "You go first, Nan."

"Thanks a lot," Nancy said cheerfully.

Holding the flashlight in one hand, she descended the ladder into the darkness.

"What's it like down there?" George asked, peering over the edge of the entrance.

"Dark. Musty," Nancy answered. She didn't mention the rat she saw skittering across the beam of the flashlight.

"I'm coming down, too," George said, climbing onto the ladder.

Nancy scanned the area around her with her light. The tunnel was large, with huge pipes suspended from the concrete ceiling. It seemed to go far into the distance, meeting up with other tunnels at both ends. "I don't see any other ladders," Nancy murmured as two more rats behind her let out a squeal and scampered away into the darkness.

"Yikes!" George cried. "Get me out of here!"

"We can't leave without Marcy," Nancy said.

George took a deep breath. "Well, which way do we go?" she asked.

"Let's try that way," Nancy said, picking a direction at random. The girls trudged down the tunnel, carefully shining the light near their feet to keep away any furry inhabitants.

Soon they came to a place where another tunnel joined the first. "I see something!" Nancy cried, running to an object in her flashlight beam.

It was a woman's gold bracelet. "That's Marcy's," George said shakily. "I remember her wearing it on the show with Dr. Helen."

"Me, too," Nancy confirmed. "Jack must have taken her this way. Let's—"

Just then a loud bang echoed through the tunnel, and Nancy felt something whiz by her ear. "Duck, George!" Nancy yelled. "He's shooting at us!"

Chapter
Fifteen

Her heart pounding, Nancy quickly switched off her flashlight, plunging the tunnel into darkness. "George! Are you okay?" Nancy whispered to her friend.

"I guess," George replied shakily.

"Get out of here!" came Jack Cole's angry voice from the darkness ahead. "Leave us alone! If you don't, I swear I'll kill her!"

"He means it, Nancy," came Marcy's terrified voice.

Nancy estimated that Marcy and Jack were about thirty feet ahead off to the right. And strangely, their voices sounded as if they were coming from someplace elevated. She squinted, and her eyes began to adjust to the dark. There was a dim light far ahead— another entrance, no doubt.

Nancy moved closer to them until she could make out Jack and Marcy's silhouettes. They were up on a catwalk, about ten feet above the ground. Nancy guessed the walk was for workers who needed access to the pipes on the ceiling of the tunnel. Marcy was in front of him, and he had an arm wrapped around her throat. In his other hand, Nancy saw the deadly shape of a pistol.

"You've convinced me, Jack," Nancy said grimly. "We're getting out of here." Making sure her footsteps sounded heavily, she began walking away.

George spun around, confused, and Nancy grabbed her arm, whispering, "Keep him involved, George. I'm going up the ladder we came down and then I'll go down that other ladder—behind them."

"Right," George whispered back. Loudly enough for Jack to hear, she said, "I'm going, too, Jack. But I wish you'd explain a few things to me before I do."

"I don't owe you or anybody an explanation," Jack growled.

"I know you don't," Nancy heard George say as she continued backing away. "But it's so amazing how you pulled this off. How did you do it?"

"It wasn't hard," Jack bragged.

"Not hard?" George said in disbelief. "To

put a bomb threat on a TelePrompTer with a studio full of people?"

A bitter laugh erupted from Jack. "That was a piece of cake," he said. "As production stage manager, I just sent everyone else off on urgent errands. I did the same thing with Brenda Fox and the detective, the day I set the fire. Karen told me how Nancy Drew had been nosing around at the magazine, so I set her up by writing a note from an intern."

As he was speaking, Nancy climbed back up the ladder, stomping loudly as she went. "George, I'm leaving," she called back after her.

"If you want Marcy dead," Jack warned, "call the police."

"I won't," Nancy yelled.

Nancy climbed out into the late afternoon sunshine. She pointed herself in the direction she knew the tunnel ran and began walking. Soon her path was blocked by a six-foot-high concrete wall. Nancy hoisted herself up onto it.

On the far side was a large parking area for track maintenance vehicles. The area appeared deserted, but at the other end of it, Nancy saw the other opening to the tunnel. It looked exactly like the one she and George had gone down. Quickly she hurried over to it. This gate, too, had been smashed open. Nancy wondered if Jack was responsible or if some other vandal had broken the lock.

She climbed down, walking stealthily so she wouldn't make any noise. As she descended, she could hear George still talking. Nancy began sneaking along the side of the tunnel, edging toward the ladder to the catwalk.

"What about the stolen sign-in sheets and signing the other one with a phony name? What was the idea of that?" George was asking.

"It was to throw you and your friend off the trail," Jack gloated. "To make you think someone had come in from outside. It worked, too!"

"You were working with Karen Kristoff, weren't you?" George was asking. "I don't understand that."

"Karen came up with the plan in the first place, but she didn't have the nerve to take it all the way," Jack said. "All she wanted was to get Marcy off the show and set herself up as the replacement. I had bigger ideas. Right, Marcy? We'll be together from now on. Now that I've rescued you from all that, you'll be able to be your real self again."

Marcy's answer was a broken sob.

"We'll be happy together," he went on, his voice an eerie whine. "Trust me. I understand you—I care about you! I may not be a big-time

143

producer like Vic Molina, but I've loved you since we were kids."

Nancy kept moving forward along the pitch-black of the side of the tunnel. Only George, who was doing a brilliant job of diverting Jack's attention, had any idea she was edging closer.

"How did you find out Nancy was investigating?" George asked him.

"I overheard the cop talking about it in the lobby after the bomb threat," Jack said. "Then I warned Nancy good. Anyone else who had seen that smashed-up mirror would have gotten off the case quick. Your friend is too stubborn. Now get out of here!"

"Wait, I'm still curious. You must have been working overtime for weeks," George said. "Were you the one who wrote the note on the back of Marcy's picture and then tore it up?"

"Yes, that was me," Jack replied. "I hate those pictures of her that make her look so glamorous. She's a regular, neighborhood girl, not the VIP everyone thinks they know. Isn't that right, Marcy?"

"Y-yes, Jack," came Marcy's terrified reply.

Nancy had climbed onto the catwalk and was almost within striking distance now. If George could just keep his attention a little bit longer . . .

"So that's why you did all this?" George asked. "For love?"

"I love Marcy, and Marcy loves me," Jack shrieked. "She doesn't realize it yet, but she will. And if she won't—well, I'll tell you one thing—that crumb Molina will never see her alive again. If I can't have her, no one will!"

"No, Jack, no," Marcy murmured. "Please, you're very sick. You need help."

Nancy silently advanced another step, coming behind Jack and Marcy.

"Shut up, Marcy!" Jack snarled. "You denied our love for so long, maybe you don't deserve to live." Nancy saw him raise the gun.

There was no time for hesitation. Swiftly, Nancy's right leg shot out, knocking Jack off balance.

"Wha— you—" he muttered through gritted teeth as he fell to his knees on the catwalk, letting go of Marcy.

"Nancy, no!" Marcy screamed. "He'll kill us both!"

Nancy couldn't turn back now. A second kick to Jack's arm knocked the gun from his hand and sent it clattering to the floor of the tunnel.

"Why, you—" Jack growled. He lunged at Nancy. Grabbing her throat hard, he made Nancy see stars as he pushed her back against the rail of the catwalk.

She couldn't breathe. He pushed harder and harder against her throat.

"Goodbye, Nancy," Jack told her through gritted teeth.

Nancy gathered all her remaining strength and kicked her leg up and into Jack's chest. He staggered backward, and by the time he'd recovered, Nancy was ready for him again. One more lightning kick sent Jack reeling back again. His head thumped hard against the concrete wall. As if in slow motion, he slid to the floor of the catwalk, where he lay in a heap, unconscious.

Still watching Jack, Nancy put out a hand to Marcy and helped her to her feet. "Nancy, thank you," Marcy murmured, clutching her hand.

George had run up to them and climbed onto the catwalk. "Is he dead, Nancy?" she asked with a shudder.

"No," Nancy answered quietly, checking Jack's pulse. "But he won't bother anybody for a while. George, help Marcy down from here, okay?" Nancy gestured for her friends to step around Jack's body.

"Listen! I hear something," George said, stopping on the rungs of the catwalk ladder.

Her eyes riveted on Jack, Nancy listened intently. A siren was getting louder.

"Thank goodness," Marcy gasped, climbing down the ladder. "The police."

Soon Lieutenant Dunne, along with about a

dozen of his officers, were clambering down the ladder into the tunnel, their powerful hand-held lights illuminating the darkness. Susan was with them.

"Anybody hurt?" the lieutenant asked, hurrying over to Nancy and the others, his men close behind.

"Only Jack Cole," Nancy told him. "He was going to kill Marcy. That's his gun down there."

"Cuff him, Phil," the man told one of the uniformed officers. "And get the ambulance people down here with a stretcher."

Jack was regaining consciousness now but lacked the strength to resist. "Are you happy, Marcy?" he asked bitterly. "Happy about what you made me do? You ruined me!"

Marcy's hand flew to her cheek as, horrified, she stepped farther away from him.

"Marcy didn't cause any of this, Jack," Nancy corrected him. "People are responsible for their own actions."

"He'll have years and years to figure all that out," the lieutenant told them. "Because this fellow will be spending a long time out of harm's way."

Following Lieutenant Dunne and the others up out of the tunnel, Nancy watched a still tearful Marcy fall into Susan's arms.

"If it weren't for Nancy and George, Susan,"

she said, gulping back tears, "I wouldn't have made it!"

"Dinner at Belmondo's. Wow!" George said, standing in Susan's entry hall.

"I have Marcy's publicity shot and a pen all ready," Nancy said, patting her shoulder bag. "Tonight we'll get that autograph for Bess."

During the day Nancy and her friends had run errands, and had even managed to go jogging along Lake Michigan before returning to Susan's apartment to change for the evening. A phone message from Lieutenant Dunne had informed them that the fingerprints on the marker had been identified as Jack's.

Now Susan stood behind Nancy and George, smoothing her glossy black hair. "Marcy is incredibly grateful, and so are the Sterns," she said.

"Well, I have no problem being treated to dinner," Nancy said cheerfully. "Everybody ready?"

The girls stepped out of the apartment and walked to Susan's car. "It's not far," Susan told them, getting in and starting the engine.

Soon Nancy and the others were entering a futuristic skyscraper to ride an elevator to the very top. Emerging from the elevator, they found themselves in an elegant restaurant with an ultramodern decor in ivory and black, with soft lighting.

"This is definitely my kind of place," George said, smiling.

"We're with the Marcy Robbins party," Nancy told the maitre d', who had stepped over to seat them.

"Yes, miss," he answered politely. "Right this way. They're in the Sun Room."

He led Nancy and her friends to a glassed-in enclosure that looked out on the whole city. Chicago's millions of lights glittered like jewels.

"Nancy!" Marcy called, standing and waving as soon as she caught sight of her. "Susan! George!"

Beaming, the talk show host greeted them all with kisses. To Nancy's surprise, Vic Molina stood beside her. He, too, greeted the girls with a warm kiss on the cheek.

"Marcy told me everything," he said appreciatively. "Thank goodness for you—all three of you."

Nancy's face must have shown surprise, because Marcy let out a laugh. "You're wondering what Vic is doing here? Well, guess what? We're dating again!"

Vic put his arm around Marcy's waist and pulled her gently toward him. "She was kind enough to forgive me for being such a jerk," he said.

Marcy smiled happily and explained, "This whole incident has really helped me to put things in perspective. It's time to get my priorities straight. Career is important, but so are the people you love."

"But you're suing her," George blurted out to Vic.

"I *was,*" he said. "But not anymore. I've dropped all claims against the show. But one of these days, if they're ever available, I'll team up with the Sterns on another project. I like the way they work." He smiled at them all. "See, nearly losing Marcy made me realize how much I really care about her."

"Speaking of the show—any news?" Susan asked with a hint of trepidation.

"Didn't I tell you? The insurance company reinstated the policy once Jack and Karen were arrested. So we start taping again next week. And guess what else? We've been extended another twenty-six weeks! The network wanted to cash in on all the publicity we've been getting."

"Marcy, that's fantastic!" Susan cried happily, giving her a hug.

"Congratulations, Marcy," Nancy chimed in. "That's great news."

"Want to hear something even wilder?" Marcy asked with a mischievous grin. "Guess who called me today, wanting to be a guest on the show again? Samantha Savage!"

"You're kidding!" George gasped.

"Isn't it incredible?" Marcy said with a giggle. "She said she never realized that having an image problem would be so good for her image! She said, 'I'm writing new music about it now. Music that'll really knock people's socks off—music with real, meaningful words.'" Everyone laughed at Marcy's dead-on impression of Samantha Savage.

"I think everyone in America will be watching when you two get together again," Nancy said as she and the others sat down at the table.

"Well," Marcy bubbled, "they're all invited to tune in."

"Before I forget, Marcy," Nancy said. "Would you sign this photo for my friend Bess?"

"With pleasure," Marcy said, taking the photo and signing it with a flourish. "And now can I have your autograph?"

"Mine?" Nancy asked, taken aback.

"Sure! You're a celebrity as far as I'm concerned," Marcy told her. "Besides, thanks to you, the hottest talk show on TV is alive and talking!"

Nancy's next case:

After catching a jewel thief in the act, Nancy hopes to steal a little time for herself. A three-day bike ride with Ned, George, and a group of Emerson College students seems the perfect escape—until a series of "accidents" puts them all on a definite downhill course. And to add insult to injury, the rider most at risk is Nancy's friend George!

But why would someone want to harm George—a girl who has never hurt anyone? Nancy knows she'll have to find answers quickly before the trip takes a dangerous detour and her friend's ten-speed spins out of control. A deadly secret has come along for the ride, and getting it out in the open may be the only way to save George's life . . . in *MOVING TARGET*, Case #87 in The Nancy Drew Files™.

THE HARDY BOYS® CASE FILES